# Head Boy

## Mark Wilson

Published by

Paddy's Daddy Publishing

Published by Paddy's Daddy Publishing.

www.facebook.com/markwilsonbooks

www.markwilsonbooks.com

Follow on Twitter: @markwilsonbooks

**Cover design by Mark Wilson**

**Look out for more great titles from Mark Wilson
on Amazon and at Paddy's Daddy Publishing**

**Also By Mark Wilson:**

Bobby's Boy
Naebody's Hero

For Sandy Stewart, who put a path before me
and gave me the confidence to take it.

Dedicated also to all the dedicated, over-worked
teachers and the present-day teachers of Bellshill
Academy who do a wonderful job. Not one of
them is a Diller.

# Acknowledgments

I'd like to thank the following people for their support in writing this novel:

Thanks to my test-readers Derek Graham, Gayle Karabelen, Colette Brown, author of *Weegie Tarot* for helping me polish the book. Thanks also to Tony Duckfield and Tony Pinnington.

Thanks also to my editor Stephanie at www.edit-my-book.com.
Steph has quite simply done an amazing job of polishing my work. I'm extremely lucky to have her, she's amazing.

Very Special thanks to Jayne Doherty and Tricia Ferguson for their continued support of my writing career. Always ready to help, your support is much appreciated and never taken for granted. Jayne in particular is ever-reliable and always ready to give an honest opinion. Thanks.

Thanks also to Keith Nixon, author of *The Fix*, for his constructive comments early in the process.

A huge thank you, as always to my wife Natalie Wilson for unwavering encouragement and support.

# Author's Note

I sat down to write the follow up to my second novel, *Naebody's Hero*. I'd begun the new book, *Somebody's Hero*, a couple of weeks before and had reached around 20,000 words. Having spent a few days researching military intelligence, I sat, intending to continue that story, decided that something else was itching my brain and opened up a fresh document.

An hour later I had the first three thousand words of the novella *Head Boy*.

I had tremendous fun writing this story, indulging the wee bit of badness in me and bringing it out as Diller.

I never intended Diller to be someone whom anyone could relate to, and certainly not someone who'd be liked as a main character. As I wrote him into existence and he began making his own decision, as all characters do at a certain point in any story, I unfortunately fell in love with the filthy, black-souled bastard. I think that the part of me that is Diller will creep out to play again at some point, soon.

This book was inspired by the music video for 'Smack my Bitch Up' by The Prodigy.

Thank you for reading my book, please consider visiting <u>Amazon.UK</u>, <u>Amazon. US</u> or <u>Goodreads</u> and leaving a review.

# Table of Contents

# SATURDAY

# 16TH JUNE, 2063

# Prologue

What a fucking joke. Here I sit in a community centre hall waiting for the guy who runs this counselling course to arrive. I'm too old for this shit, but here I am, waiting for Collin, whom I met for the first time about an hour ago.

Collin Bottomley. There's a target's name if ever one was invented. I can absolutely guarantee you that this guy's tardiness isn't due to his being in the bathroom combing his hair or adjusting his clothing with loving pride. Collin is a loser's loser. Dressed baldy-head to athlete's-foot-infected toe in Matalan's finest polyester, Collin emanates beige through his every pore. From his Crocs and socks combo (beige) to his wee pocket protector that valiantly holds his pens and protects his short-sleeved shirt pocket from any wayward ink, every fibre of this guy screams out "I'm a forty-year-old man who shares a bath with my mother and still wets the bed". Even his haircut looks like a tea-towel-over-the-shoulders, pudding-bowl-on-the-head, mother's cut. I can imagine the kids in his street making his life a misery, throwing toilet paper at his house and chasing him down the road calling him some imaginative nickname. Wee kids are good at those.

The community centre I've been sent to for this 'session' is permeated with the stench of poor people, babies, incontinence, Dettol, shite and death. I spot the leftovers of a poorly cleaned shite-stain on the wall by the door and peer closer to make out the faded message written in excrement, long ago cleaned (poorly) but still visible.

## Wullie shat here

I sit wondering if Wullie delivered his writing material fresh into his hand before leaving his touching prose or if he brought his shite, wrapped neatly in some newspaper, ready for his next artistic project. I'm finding it difficult enough to believe that I have to attend this meaningless session without having to read Wullie's philosophical musings whilst I wait for my counsellor. I mean, anger management for fuck sake.

I only came back to Scotland for a flying visit. A quick in and out, to check up on young Michael Bosanko, who runs my business for me these days; does a good job of it too. *Clever lad that one.* There I was, putting my smoke-free cigarette in my mouth for a wee nicotine hit, and *she* starts her pish.

Airline stewardesses have always been a tricky proposition, but I've honestly lost track of what you're allowed, or not allowed, to do/say/think in public anymore; especially on flights. *You'll have to put that out, Mr Diller,* she told me. What the fuck is there to put out with an electronic cig? Apparently some people are averse to watching someone else smoke, even fake-smoke, so the airline banned it on all flights. *Even fuckin' first class?* I asked. That was it. In cuffs by an air-marshal, in front of a justice of the fuckin' peace and sent for anger management; for smoking an electronic fag, and swearing at some torn-faced slapper. Christ, if old Hondo were around to see me now, arrested for this pish.

This Collin's late. I can't stand lateness and I've hurt people for less. That was in the past though. I'm respectable these days. This Collin-cunt obviously thinks I've got nothing else to be doing but wait on this plastic-covered social incompetent deciding which coloured pen he'll be using to note down my deficiencies and/or progress before coming to meet me.

Of course, I'm aware that it's just part of the process, a test to see if I can be patient. I can, on the outside. Inside I'm raging; I could've had my business completed and be halfway back to the airport by now in the time I've spent here sitting staring at the formerly cheery, faded purple woodchip walls adorned with quite literally the shittiest graffiti man could produce.

When he does get here, this Collin, I'll nod, look thoughtful and agree that I really should think things through before I act. I'll tell him that I've been really upset since the incident and have thought of nothing other than how to make amends to that poor girl. I'll say all the things he wants to hear, tick all his 'the patient has seen that his actions have consequence and feels regret, the patient exhibits normal responses to stress' boxes and get the fuck out of here before this wee dick decides that he wants to be my boyfriend. Imagine if my boys saw me sitting here with this wee fanny spewing phrases like "Thanks, Collin, that's a big help" or "Yes, Collin, I see how that technique would be of huge benefit to me" through a haze of red hatred. Not that Collin would spot the venom in me; he's lapping up my act of penitence, my grief. This guy lives to be needed, to be useful, to 'fix' people. What a fuckin' loser.

Guys like Collin are all the same. They take comfort in the belief that people like me have a wall up around our emotions; that we don't know any better or don't understand that it's all right to mourn or cry or care. We do, but we just don't give a shit. We hate the weak, who sit and bleat about how they feel.

Collin and his type believe that with education or therapy we can be 'assisted'; we can be fixed. We can't, or more accurately, we won't. Here's the truth. People like me enjoy being bad bastards. It's quite simply great fun for us and we love how incomprehensible our actions seem to you. To us, you, the normal folk are the walking dead and a source of endless amusement, to be manipulated, used and discarded by me and mine as the whim takes us. Discuss your feelings all you like, I'll be sitting pishing myself at how much of a pussy you are, whilst painting a sympathetic expression on my face. I've lived to a ripe old age and never once have I done a damn thing I didn't want to do. How many of us can say that? Especially in this day and age.

Collin and his type take comfort in the belief that guys like me have demons lurking, that we don't know ourselves. Not true; I had a wonderful childhood. No deep-seeded angst hidden under my 'fuck you' attitude. No hidden pain forged in the furnace of some creepy uncle's or some priest's unwanted sexual attentions. No divorced parents or violent incidents or sibling rivalry or any of that shite. Nope, no one tampered with me or beat me or called me useless or put unrealistic pressures on me to succeed or ignored me or over-indulged me; I was disciplined fairly and consistently by two parents who loved me and each other unconditionally. An ideal childhood really.

My mum was a teacher and, whilst I loved my old Mammy, I can't stand teachers. What a bunch of self-important wankers the teaching profession is riddled with. These people spend so much of their time talking down to those in their charge, that a thin-lipped scowl and accusatory stare over reading glasses perched at the end of their alcoholic noses are as standard on most teachers' faces as the ubiquitous mug of coffee is in their hands and the nicotine stains on their trembling fingers. It's impossible for some-one like me to take a teacher seriously. Most of these people are straight out of school into university, back into school again, and they stand there with a straight face giving the young team advice on how to *succeed* in life. They ain't ever lived one, a real, full life that is, but it doesn't stop them from telling other folk what they should be doing with theirs. Honestly, it's like a nun giving Sex-Ed to a hooker.

Dad was the only thing worse than a teacher; a fucking copper. Good guy though my old man... for a copper.

It's true that I had a very ordinary and, if I'm be-ing honest, boring early childhood. Happily for me and my monochrome wee world, I discovered by the age of around nine that I find great enjoyment in fucking with and fucking over people at every opportunity. Vandalism, kidnapping and shaving small family pets, urinating in letter boxes; all innocent enough fun for a lad and a great way to learn the trade. By my teenage years, violence was my life. I was an experienced torturer of the general populace with a vast array of strategies at my disposal, each designed to bring a little misery into my chosen victim's day and a wee smile to my lips. Small victories or great big fuck-off ones, I took my fun where I could.

Everyone was fair game for my attentions. Pensioners, kids, teachers, polis; all provided me with my fun over the years. I'm usually pretty careful to maintain a sweet exterior, though. I'm a fly bastard y'see. Never got caught. That bastard Bowie though, he got close.

The bottom line is that no matter what I say to Collin in this shite-sprayed room, I'm not feeling the things he expects me to feel. I don't want to change and no great tragedy has made me this way. I choose to do the things I do because it gives me a thrill to watch daft cunts squirm, and it always has. The incident on the plane though, that was fuck-all. Is that all it takes these days to be a criminal, to deserve rehabilitation, to insult some wee lassie in the First

Class section of an aeroplane by using the word 'fuck'?

As I look across at Collin, the old me stirs. He's been dulled significantly by decades of luxury and food and alcohol and a thousand lovers, but he's still there, and I sorely want to let the bastard out to play with Collin.

Just being in Scotland brings back the memories and the thrill of being him, of being who I was, rushing back with the kick of an elephant's-leg line of coke. Heart thumping, I watch Collin and try to satisfy the urge by dredging up the memories of those times. The good times.

\*\*\*\*\*\*\*\*\*\*\*\*

# MONDAY

# Chapter 1

## The Academy

Strutting along Bellshill main street Davie Diller kicked a discarded Coke can under the wheels of a buggy, causing one of the rear tyres to suffer a slash as it crushed the can beneath it. It was unintended but Diller took satisfaction from the sound of the tyre bursting anyway. The young mum, fag in hand, black leggings-cum-tights straining to contain her blubbery legs, continued, oblivious to the puncture.

As he neared Bellshill Academy, Diller took a hard drag on what remained of his cigarette and tossed it with a flick at the heels of a pensioner who faced away from him. Today Diller didn't need the hassle that being seen smoking near the school grounds brought, he had enough on his plate. Dressed in denims, shirt and tie and wearing a new pair of Adidas Superstar 2 trainers, Diller shoved his way through the double doors of the formerly *boys only* entrance. He fully expected a few snide comments about his appearance from some of the staff, but his attitude unsurprisingly was *fuck 'em.* Diller figured that the teachers would love to have the balls to turn up in school in decent attire instead of their ubiquitous, black shoes, troos, and ever-so-rebellious Wal-Mart patterned shirt and tie combo.

"Haw, wee-man." Diller grabbed tightly on the arm of a third year he'd spotted hanging about at the door. "You better have something for me."

Terror filling his eyes, the pupil stared nervously up at Diller. "Aye, I mean, yes. It's here…"

"Right. Good." Diller cut him off by snatching the small envelope the kid was offering out of his hand. Pocketing it and pushing the boy aside, he painted a cheery smile on his face as Mr Oliphant passed. "Morning Mr Oliphant," Diller sing-songed at the passing Maths teacher.

Fumbling around in his briefcase, Oliphant, dressed in a tragic turquoise Asda shirt and tie combo didn't manage to look up but grunted a distracted, "Morning."

Diller shook his head, wondering, not for the first time, how a dozy old bastard like Olly managed to remember how to breathe in and out all day, never mind explain complex equations to his pupils. At least he had a nice way with him, old Olly, unlike the majority of the arsehole teaching staff. Smiling to himself, Diller continued upstairs towards the English department and his first class.

"Morning Mr Diller." Never far from the English department, Mr Bowie loomed at the end of the corridor. He had a gift for making a friendly morning greeting sound like an accusation. He made *Mr Diller* sound like *arsehole.*

Davie had been in Bowie's class in fifth year. It'd been one hell of a year. Bowie was never off his back, a total head case. The simplest mistake or misspelling, or breathing too loud some days, was enough to tip the man over the edge and into a rant about *responsibility, carelessness etc.* Obviously, this meant that Bowie was by far the best teacher in school to rip the pish out of, but Davie had learned to be circumspect in his efforts; no use giving him fuel for the fire of his outrage. Besides, in a school with seventy-odd teachers, Bowie was the only one who had seen past Davie's outer persona. Right from their first encounter he'd stared right through the intelligence, manners and faux-charm, straight into the devious and dangerous little shite who lived beneath the veneer of a dedicated pupil. Imagine Bowie's joy when, in sixth year, as a reward for all of his 'consistently excellent contributions to the school', Diller was made Head Boy.

Bowie seemed to have been a teacher at Bellshill Academy forever. An ex-Royal Marine he'd had the occasional recall to the services during large-scale conflicts. He'd taught the parents of a lot of the kids in Diller's class, and he was still here, having not evolved to the changing times one iota. How the hell can a teacher from the late seventies hope to understand what goes on in the mind of kids in the year 2013? With iPads, Kindles, the internet – hell, indoor toilets – it must be like the future to a guy like Bowie.

Dressed in a brown tweed suit, beige shirt, brown tie, green pullover and tan-coloured shoes, Bowie also sported the only two things that could possibly have marked him out even further as a man displaced from his own time: a great big, bushy, grey moustache and a Beatles-style bright ginger toupee. The fact that Bowie was onto him from first glance, combined with his appearance and the old man's attempts to control him, quite simply made Bowie an irresistible target to Diller.

As Diller wasn't late today, for once, that meant that he was probably overdue with an assignment. Without stopping, Diller pushed his way into the classroom and disappeared through the door, pretending he hadn't heard. *Prick*

*First one here*, Diller noted as he entered the ancient-looking and smelling classroom. The wood panelled walls bore the carvings of generations of Bellshill Academy pupils: 'BYT', 'Linda gies gobbles' and other such displays of wit adorned the panels. The painted sections above the wood had faded from bright white to dark brown over the decades. The polystyrene ceiling tiles, dotted with precariously hanging pencils and spit-formed balls of paper towel fragments, added no ambience.

Taking his customary chair at the rear of the room, Diller stretched his legs, lifting them up and onto his desk and pulled his phone out to check on his Facebook page as he waited for the classroom to fill up. *There's wee Stacey sent me a message. She's a wee dirty, that yin. Probably after her hole.*

Jabbing on the envelope icon to open the message, Diller confirmed his suspicions as to the contents of Stacey's message. 'U up 4 it the night, Davie?' and quickly closed it again without replying, preferring to keep his options open. Tonight was a long way off; anything could happen between now and then. It was a school night, sure, but Angel's in Uddingston had a three-hour happy hour tonight and it was calling his name.

Stacey, twenty-one-year-old receptionist at Cardinal Newman High, across the other end of town, had been a fuck-buddy of his for around six months. She was sound as fuck. Always around when he took the notion; never needy for a wee cuddle or a kind word afterwards. They had to keep their liaisons quiet at any rate, due to the age difference. Diller suspected that Stacey was as bad as he was when it came to her attitude towards sexual partners, seeing them as little more than sex-aids. That was fine by him. A wicked grin crossed Diller's face as he enjoyed a quick mental flashback to their last encounter together at her modest flat on Main Street. *Christ! That was a good night.*

Enjoying the afterglow of the memory, he re-opened the message and replied.

;-).

Sometimes words got you into trouble so a non-committal winking emoticon would keep those gates open without promising anything.

Just as Diller moved to thumb the off button, a significantly less welcome message vibrated through.

Moving his finger to open it, Diller's heart sank at the name that appeared. Big Hondo.

Big Hondo was actually James Crosbie of Babylon Road. Sixty-eight years old with the muscle mass of a man half his age, Big Hondo stood well over six feet in height. A former steelworker, in the 90s Hondo had used his substantial redundancy money to set himself up at the forefront of the only thriving business Thatcher had left in the area, the drug business. Hondo had also had the foresight and intelligence to attend university, using the re-training wage kindly offered to the redundant men of Ravenscraig by Mrs T, graduating with a 2:1 in Business Management.

Hondo attacked his new venture with the same commitment he had shown at Uni. With the single-minded fastidiousness that only mature students bring, he implemented his detailed business plan; making a vast number of contacts abroad, establishing a supply chain, examining the logistics of his new enterprise, building a network of mules and street-corner/club dealers, armed with bags of... whatever. Hondo quite literally carved himself a huge slice of the drug trade pie in North and South Lanarkshire. In the process he employed violence more often than he employed new dealers.

Most folk in the area believed he gained the nickname 'Hondo' due to his love of all things Western-related. Permanently dressed in double-denim, cowboy boots, belt and Stetson, Hondo wasn't difficult to spot in The Orb, a local pub, of an evening. The truth was that Hondo acquired his nickname from his enthusiastic use of the Bowie knife, a cowboy's favourite blade, as his preferred deal-maker and deal-breaker. Taking all of five years, Hondo had slashed, stabbed, throttled, drowned, bought, shagged, bribed, murdered and dealt his way to a position of power that had ultimately made him untouchable in Lanarkshire. Rumour had it that he had a fair few cops on his payroll, which Diller's dad said was rubbish. *Drug-dealer propaganda* he'd called it. Whatever the truth was, when it came to scoring some top-notch Charlie, Hondo was the man in Lanarkshire – and the man was not to be fucked with. *So they said.*

Working with Big Hondo was Wee Hondo, or Lionel, his son. Wee Hondo was, if anything, even bigger than his Dad, but had none of the old man's fierce intelligence. The only ferocity he displayed was with his fists. Growing up with Hondo as his father, immersed in the old man's business, had made the boy as hard as rock. Since he didn't need to be clever, not with the old boy running things, Wee Hondo was best utilised in the more physical side of the business. He was good at it and enjoyed its challenges immensely.

Over the years, Wee Hondo had developed a reputation as a skilled remover of body parts. He could remove pretty much anything from a person whilst avoiding his victim bleeding out, or so they said. A true chip off the old, blade-wielding, gonad-smashing block that was Big Hondo. It was true that the apple didn't fall far from the tree, but in Hondo's case it had fallen with a pair of size fourteen, steel toe-capped boots, a pre-disposition towards torture and an evil grin.

The trio was competed by Big Hondo's dad, a wheelchair-bound ninety year old who smoked all day, dispensed larger deals to more *trusted clients* who visited their home and never left the house.

The Crosbies weren't the only drug-dealers in the small former-mining town but the three men controlled a continuous flow of the highest quality cocaine in a twenty mile radius and oversaw the activities of the others. Generously, the Crosbies also offered 'tic', an arrangement where the purchaser could obtain the drug of their choice gratis for an arranged period, usually a week or two. After that it was pay up or lose body parts, courtesy of Wee Hondo. Diller was normally the type who preferred the former payment plan, but had been taking the piss recently, bringing him dangerously close to paying the latter price.

Looking back to his phone, Diller sat staring at the unopened icon for a few minutes. *Shit.* Whatever Hondo wanted wouldn't be good news,that Diller was certain of. He thumbed the message and felt a shiver pass through his muscles as he read the words 'Hundred Grand by Friday or UR dead'.

# Chapter 2

## On a School Night

"Give me those fags." Diller had a scraggy-looking fourth-year boy, whose name he didn't know and who had a squint in his eye, pressed against the wall in the alcove under the assembly hall.

"Ye cannae dae that," the wee guy squealed.

Diller poked an index finger into 'Skelly-eye's' shoulder. "Hurry up ya wee fanny." His voice was calm and quiet. Skelly-eye looked around at his friends for a bit of back-up, but they'd picked a spot each on the ground to study and were avoiding Diller's challenging, scanning stare. One of them got a moment of courage and told Skelly-eye, "Just give him them, Jordan."

Diller pushed his nose closer to Jordan's. Letting some gas rise up his throat, he belched loudly in the kid's face, noticing the after-burn of the cold curry he'd had for breakfast. Jordan retched a little at the smell and reached into his jacket pocket for his ten-deck of Lambert and Butler.

"Here." Jordan slapped the pack into Diller's waiting hand.

"Smoking's bad for ye, Jordan," Diller put a mocking tone into the name. "I'm doing you a favour here, son. Right," he leaned in close to whisper into Jordan's ear, "get tae fuck, dick."

As the little group of fourth years ran off, Diller rounded the corner and entered the bin shed, flicking one of Jordan's cigarettes into his mouth as he walked out of view. Grimacing at the first harsh lungful, he examined the silver box Jordan had given him. *Cheap, shitey fags, I'll have to pick a better class of loser for my next pack.*

Lunchtime lasted fifty minutes and Diller normally spent that time smoking in the bin shed, chatting up some of the sixth-year lassies or occasionally doing some work in the library to keep up appearances. Today, he smoked eight of the ten cigarettes Jordan had 'gifted' him in a twenty-minute blast, mind racing with possibilities, consequences and possible outcomes. This thing with Hondo was a worry, no doubt about it.

A long-term client and worker of Hondo's, Diller had made a small business of buying manageable quantities of coke over the last two years or so. He had a small number of guys dealing for him, after a wee tamper with the quality of the product, of course, and with Hondo's blessing. The problem was that over the last six months or so, Diller had taken on an absolute mountain of coke, all on 'tic' and with a far too care-free attitude.

He hadn't snorted a hundred grands' worth of Hondo's Charlie on his own; he found that coke made him a bit too careless and made his ego grow out of control. On the contrary, he'd been very generous with it. The coke had been meted out to barmen, bouncers and potential sexual partners, to low-level dealers whose own inferior product paled in comparison and any number of thugs over the six months.

Diller was building his own wee network of 'friends' and filling an account full of favours owed from a range of useful types around Lanarkshire. You never knew when an alibi, some muscle, entry to a club or some sex would be needed and Diller liked to keep a myriad of opportunities and options on call. School, with its ever-changing clientele and flow of people, was an ideal recruiting base and networking opportunity for those who kept their eyes open. Never dealing though, not in school.

It was an expensive endeavour, this networking and favour gathering, and one that Hondo had been happy to fund, in the short-term, owing to Diller's connections to the constabulary through his dad and the impressive sales he'd clocked up over a short time. It looked like Hondo had either decided that Diller had been giving away too much or not selling enough, or that Diller was gaining too large a network and wanted him shut down. There was also the possibility that Hondo simply wanted a return on his investment. A *hundred grand, though? Surely Hondo's been a bit heavy on the interest there, I couldn't have done in that much coke in six months, could I?*

Lighting cigarette number nine, Diller noted that it was the 'lucky fag' from the packet, the one that everyone always turns filter side down when a fresh pack is opened. Smiling in acknowledgment at the absurdity of the ubiquitous smoker's habit, he sparked it up. As he smoked his way down to the shite at the end of the cigarette, almost to the filter, an evil smile spread across his face and a plan tickled the cold recesses of his brain. *It'd be tricky, but it just might work.*

Flicking the butt into the pile he'd made, Diller straightened his shirt and headed up to the assembly hall as the bell rang, signalling that lunchtime was over. As part of his 'Special Duties' he regularly delivered a short motivational or informative speech at some of the junior kids' assemblies. It was fourth year today and a talk on health and wellbeing. Diller would be advising the junior pupils on the evils of drugs, alcohol and smoking. To be fair, he wasn't exactly short of experience on the subjects. He'd have to remember to 'thank' Jordan for his lucky fag if he saw him in assembly.

Leaving the school grounds within ten minutes of the final bell ringing, Diller turned off of Main Street, passed Riley's pool hall, which was in the process of closing for good, and walked along Thorn Road towards the railway bridge. Having grabbed a Superdry hoodie from his school locker, Diller pulled the hood up over his head. His old man still worked in the police station. He rode a desk these days, but still had a finger in every pie. Diller needed to slip past unnoticed. He could do without a conversation with the old man at the moment; he had places to be.

Continuing along towards the little tunnel under the bridge, he slipped through and took the short walk to 'The Sandy', a shitehole of a park where all the local Neds gathered. One Ned in particular interested him, Tommy McTavish, aka Tawttie.

Tawttie appeared with a small crew of his 'team', a bunch of local losers who Diller had known for years. Each of them had been a pupil at Bellshill Academy.

Noticing Diller lurking on the periphery of the park, Tawttie left his four comrades and shuffled over in Diller's direction. Dressed in typical NED attire of tracksuit, trousers tucked into socks, scabby-looking, mud-ingrained white clothes offset by sparkling white trainers, Burberry cap and a brace of sovereign rings, Tawttie and his crew looked like every other wee fanny in Lanarkshire. Their clothes were practically a uniform and the trademark 'dug', normally a Rottweiler or Pit-bull, was a given.

Not being the academic type, Tawttie had left Bellshill Academy in fourth year and been quickly recruited by Diller. Amongst other things, he couriered items and substances, but essentially did Diller's dirty work for him, allowing Diller to maintain his facade. The pair had first spoken business after a particularly vicious playground fight that Tawttie had won quickly and clinically with a boot to the balls and a stamp on the prone head of his opponent. Diller had watched with interest as Tawttie had dismantled the other boy, moving aside only as Bowie pushed past him to break up the fight, admonishing Diller with a hard stare for standing and watching the display. Within a week of the incident, Tawttie was permanently expelled from school and working for Diller.

Guys like Tawttie were far from rare in Lanarkshire and easily made use of; a few free bags of Charlie here, a few quid there, some opportunities to make some easy money and build a bit of a street-rep. They weren't interested in getting a job; all they wanted was some money, and some drugs in their pocket and their hole occasionally.

Fear was another excellent tool to make these guys comply and one which Diller was expertly skilled in wielding. Physically, any one of these guys could easily overcome Diller, but he'd been patient in his younger days. Overheard conversations between his dad and a variety of colleagues, greasing the right palms with drugs and money, the threat of Hondo in his corner – these things had served to place Diller into a position where these street-mugs respected and feared him. As the son of a teacher and a copper, convention would dictate that he'd be the last type of guy to involve himself in this world. His desires, connections, insight, skills, ambition and inherent badness had made him a natural.

By far the most difficult part to date had been keeping up his mask of normality in school and at home, but he'd turned it into a game in his mind, considering the roles he played as his secret identity – like Batman, but a bastard-Batman. Every so often though, violence was required by circumstances and demanded by his true self, the pressure of hiding his inner bastard built up and needed to be released.

He'd learned to pick his moment over the years and selected people that no one would miss; those who would serve as a warning to others. Junkies, dealers, people who owed dealers money, nobodies. He always cleaned up after himself, burning every fibre of clothing he may have worn in the act as well as his victim's remains. Each kill attributed, on the grape-vine, to Wee Hondo.

Of course, with Tawttie, there was the added incentive that the guy had seen the monster hidden under the mask when he'd walked into a dark close on Lawmuir Road in the early hours to find Diller crouched over a forty-year-old man, knife in his eye socket, eye on the ground. No stranger to cutting a man himself, Tawttie had nodded, turned around silently and left Diller to his work, but he'd never looked at him directly again and never argued when issued a task. The incident, some time ago, had shown Tawttie who and what he was working for.

"Eh, awright, eh… Diller." Tawttie's voice was nasal and he used exaggeratedly long and faux cheery notes, again part of the NED persona. He was nervous; he always was around Diller. This showed that he was smarter than he looked.

Diller ignored Tawttie's eloquent greeting and threw a fifty-gram bag of Charlie in his direction. The coke, Hondo's finest, was cut generously with glucose from the school's Science stores and cost Tawttie one hundred pounds per gram. Diller had 'paid' Hondo eighty pounds for it. The effective downgrading of the

Charlie made it go a whole lot further and usually went unnoticed by the kind of mutant who opted to purchase their drugs from the likes of Tawttie. His clientele would still be thrilled at the quality despite the glucose; it would most likely be a nice change from their nose-powder being cut with bathroom products. In all likelihood, when Tawttie's coke made its way down the supply chain a few levels, from the odd banker and lawyer to Hipsters, bored housewives and deadbeats, it'd probably still be destined to mingle with a variety of household powders until the junky at the bottom of the pile and the peak of some junk withdrawal was snorting about one percent coke, ninety-nine percent fuck-knows-what.

"Money," Diller barked at Tawttie who hurriedly fished a scabby-looking brown bag stuffed with what Diller expected would be even scabbier-looking notes of all denominations from one of his pockets and placed it in Diller's hand.

At that, Diller left without another word and headed to five more similarly engaging appointments with several variations on Tawttie around town. The money was stacking up, for sure, but a hundred grand in a week was unlikely. That was the whole point. Hondo liked to make an example of someone from time to time. It was becoming apparent that Diller's moment had arrived. It seemed that Hondo had abandoned his corner and become his opponent. Despite the precarious position that Diller was now in, he smiled to himself at the thought of the coming storm.

*Bring it on, Hondo.*

# Chapter 3

## I'm Lovin' Angel's…

"How's it goin', Stevie?" Slipping a wrap of coke into the bouncer's palm, Diller shook his hand enthusiastically.

"Great, Davie. You keeping busy, are ye?" Stevie disengaged from the greeting and covertly slipped the wrap into his trouser pocket.

"You know me, Stevie. I'm always busy." Diller nodded towards the pub's door. "All the usuals in tonight?" What he was really asking was if Hondo was around.

"Aye, a good crowd in tonight, Davie," Stevie replied. "I'll give ye a shout if need be, awright?"

Diller relaxed a little and brightened at the prospect of a carefree (and hopefully profitable) night in Angel's bar. "Thanks Stevie, see you later, eh?"

"Aye, have a good one, son." Stevie turned back to the street, but quickly whipped his head back around. "Hang on Davie, how's yer old man doing?"

Stevie had once been Detective Sergeant Steven Miller and had worked under DCI Douglas Diller in the local CID, the force's serious crimes division. Teammates for years, Stevie and Dougie had been founding members of the Bellshill CID's Drug Squad and had been vital in limiting Hondo's expansion into South Lanarkshire. During a particularly violent arrest, Stevie had been stabbed in the thigh. The blade, severing his femoral artery and damaging the motor nerves to his left leg, had ended his career. As well as almost bleeding out and sustaining irreparable nerve damage, Stevie had suffered from PTSD ever since. Unsupported by the police force and treated mostly with scorn for his mental health problems, Stevie had never again been the same man, which had turned out to be a stroke of luck for Davie.

Douglas had seen to it that Stevie was offered a desk-job at Motherwell headquarters, but Stevie, disillusioned and embittered by his experiences, had opted to take early medical retirement. A bitter ex-copper with a limp and a grudge against most of his former colleagues, a shite pension and invaluable insider knowledge of both the police and Hondo's organisation had been a major boost for Davie's plans.

"Aye, he's good thanks, Stevie, still working away." Diller noted a pang of sadness cross the older man's face.

"Aye, good guy, Dougie is. Tell him I'm asking after him." Stevie turned his attention to a wee NED. Pished out of his skull and falling towards the big ex-copper, the wee guy had no chance of being admitted to Angel's that night.

Diller gave Stevie a friendly punch on the upper arm from behind and headed inside.

Scanning the bar and the dance floor as he entered, Diller confirmed Stevie's assertion that all the usual faces were indeed present. Angel's in Uddingston had been open for business for decades but the owners had kept the place well decorated and the riff-raff out. Always lively, the venue also benefitted from a steady stream of barely-legal and slightly under-age cider-drinkers from Bellshill. As such, there were always a few fifth and sixth-years from Bellshill Academy in during the week. After noting the faces around the room, Diller grinned, enjoying the discomfort his presence brought to some of the faces in the bar who knew him well enough. Acknowledging their stares with a nod, to convey *Aye, I've seen ye*, Diller slid his eyes to the corner booths and his feet followed.

The particular booth he'd selected was habitually occupied with his kind of people. Ranging from nineteen to twenty-five years old, cash on the hip and mostly women, these were very definitely his target market. Part of the group he'd been buttering up for the last few months, these folk now spent a fortune on Charlie. University students, trainee lawyers and bankers and the odd high-class prossie, they were young, full of themselves, horny and had money to burn. Whenever Diller joined their company, he was welcomed with open arms. These guys got their coke at two hundred quid a gram from Diller and as such got it uncut. They paid top price and got top quality, and this kept them coming back. For these guys, Diller took the risk of holding a prosecutable amount of coke.

"Hey, David. Sooo great to see you." The blonde, Maxine, got up and air-kissed both of his cheeks. Diller hated that insincere bullshit and noted it down as another reason to dislike Maxine. He had plenty already; from her extensions, to her make-up, to her annoying middle-class tones and equally 'educated' opinions, Maxine bored him rigid. Still, he often found that the more he despised women, the more fun he had when he was having sex with them. Diller knew that some guys only shagged people they liked, or even loved. He was exactly the opposite, never happier in the act than when he hated the object of his lust. *Maxine might be a contender tonight.*

"Hiya, Maxine." Diller gave her his most sincere, most dazzling smile, the one he'd practiced for hours to get right. His own natural smile had been just too filthy, too predatory, and he'd had to work hard to affect a more genuinely warm one when the company demanded it. Sitting down he flashed his best smile again and passed more kisses and handshakes around the table.

Around the table in front of him were five up-and-comers. Maxine, of course, tall, blonde, not an original thought in her head but somehow one of the most sought-after legal trainees in her graduating class.

Gerry 'fuckin' Malone was also in tonight. A banker, Gerry had left school at sixteen and gone straight into corporate banking, spending five years grafting his way to a solid associate director's position. Gerry's type, uneducated wide-boy, was prevalent in the corporate banking world, and whilst a good laugh, Gerry was a wee bit too fond of telling people around him how great he was to be taken seriously. He also had a habit of talking about himself in the third person, sprinkling the words 'fuck' or 'fuckin'' liberally throughout sentences. *Gerry's fuckin' hungry. This fuckin' coke is right fuckin' up Gerry's fuckin' street, by fuck.* It was funny for about fifteen minutes and then became an exercise in patience for Diller, who often dreamed of palming Gerry's 'fuckin' nose through Gerry's 'fuckin' brain. He was too good a customer, though. At the moment.

The only other body at the table who Diller knew much about was Mary Murphy, and what a body. Twenty-one, redheaded and studying to be a doctor, Mary had so far resisted Diller's charms. Mary could snort as much coke as she could afford, which was a lot, but showed no interest in the carnal pursuits; not with Diller at any rate. Starting to dislike her for her lack of interest in him, Diller was becoming obsessed with the idea of getting her into bed, or anywhere else he could manage.

The other two seemed of the same ilk. No real surprises or interest there, but he'd charm and schmooze away with them and see if they were any use to him.

Inevitably in this company, the conversation was money, status and property-focused with only the occasional detour into a topic that even half-interested Diller. On the up-side, the coke kept everyone confidently talking loudly, no matter how little they actually had to say.

"Oh I always download my music from iTunes." Maxine had been going on about the evils of piracy of music and movies. "They're a little expensive, sure, but I think that it's good to support the artists. Don't you, David?"

Formed from a few half-read articles in *The Mail*, *Heat* and *OK! Magazine* and from listening to judges on TV talent shows, Maxine's opinions always reminded Diller that for some people, being educated was a far cry from being clever or being capable of forming a single independent thought. This was her most nonsensical rant yet and had Diller struggling to hide his disdain. Almost every word she over-enunciated on the subject made him want to scream at her.

In Diller's mind, and the minds of most at his school, only the most ridiculously moronic would actually pay for music or films, or books for that matter. Especially books, they give the things away for Christ sake.

"How right you are, Maxine. I feel the same way," he schmoozed. "Tell me, which *artists* are you *supporting* at the moment?" Diller barely succeeded in keeping the malicious sarcasm from his tone.

Maxine wafted her hand over the table in a dismissive gesture, but still managed to look smugly around. "Oh, I simply love Taylor Swift and One Direction. I buy everything by them."

Looking suitably impressed with Maxine's high moral approach to the arts and her compassion for the artistic plebs, Diller stood up and headed to the bar to buy drinks for the table and to release some expletives out of earshot.

Despite Maxine's insufferable moments, the night passed in a blur. Noticing Gerry 'fuckin'' Malone scratch his nose as a signal, Diller rose from the booth and headed to a deal in the bathroom, accepting a double vodka, no ice, from a mate on the way. Whilst there he shared a fat line with Gerry.

"Gerry's fuckin' happy noo," Gerry announced as he left the cubicle.

*Good for fuckin' you* Diller thought as he took a seat on the toilet pan, drained his vodka glass and lit a cig, ignoring the *no smoking* signs.

The rest of the night passed in a frenzy of sales, beer, a quick, unsatisfying fumble with Maxine in the disabled toilet, some dancing and farewells, come two am. He'd had worse nights in the past, that was for sure, but he'd had better ones too. The group had bought ten grams throughout the night, with Gerry fuckin' Malone stocking up for a business trip to London. It was a start, but it was still a long route to Hondo's hundred grand.

Saying goodbye to Stevie at the door and slipping him a hundred quid, Diller intended to head home for the night when a message beeped through on his phone from Stacey.

'You up for it?'

Diller thought for all of half a second before deciding, *it's a school-night, but fuck it,* and thumbing in his reply. 'Where?'

A picture of Stacey's tits popped through with the message, 'Picnic bench, down The Glen'. Diller laughed and signalled a black cab. *Dirty cow.*

Mark Wilson

# Chapter 4

## Hondo

"Right, son, come and lift this for me." Hondo patted the top of a cube of tightly cling-filmed cash that was straining his desk top. "Yer Da's getting too old to be humphing weights like this around."

Sighing, his boy took a few seconds to finish his current attack on Fifa '14 before pausing the game and strolling over to his father's desk. "Where ye wanting it, Da? Basement?"

Big Hondo smiled warmly at his son, "Please, Lionel." Watching his lad scoop up the stack of cash and effortlessly sweep it downstairs to the basement, Big Hondo chuckled at both the money and with pride in his big, strong laddie. *He might spend a bit too much time sitting on his arse playing X-box for a thirty year old, but his strength, enthusiasm for a scrap and dedication to his family mean he's a credit to his Da and a great business partner,* he mused, curling the end of his droopy moustache thoughtfully.

Big Hondo did worry occasionally about how effectively his son would be able to run the business once he was no longer around to give guidance and direction. Lionel wasn't exactly gifted in the brains department, but Hondo had been forced to put that to the back of his mind, at least for the time being.

The Diller boy had looked like a good prospect up until a few months ago, but the cheeky wee bastard was taking far too many liberties of late. Davie was a clever one, for sure, and patient with it. The boy had a natural affinity for the deal and for networking and greasing the right palms. He also possessed a gift for keeping his hand in but his name out of their dark world. Hondo found it simply astounding how great a front Diller had put up and maintained for those around him over the years.

The son of a respected secondary school teacher and one of the hardest, straightest cops in the area, most people viewed young Diller through admiring and expectant eyes. Dedicated, clever, charming, a bright future ahead, rarely did anyone who walked in the daytime world notice Diller's other side: the real Diller. It was no easy task to disguise oneself so effectively, especially when such a motivated and sadistic little shit lurked beneath the disguise. Most folk could spot such badness; the danger emanating from that type of individual. In most cases, the creep would either be spotted instinctively or else the sadistic, violent part would get cocky and let the mask slip once too often. Hondo had to hand it to the boy.

He was infallible, the finest actor the old businessman had ever seen.

The single most admirable trick Diller had pulled, though, was in maintaining his anonymity. Despite doing deals all over Lanarkshire, controlling half a dozen or so street dealers and partying with the Hooray Henrys, nobody seemed to have a clue what Diller really was. That was quite a feat in these days of social media where everyone's business from their dinner to their holidays was all over the Tweet-box or on Facebook for all to see.

None of that admiration meant that Diller could be allowed to continue as he had been. Hondo had been happy to support him in building his network of dealers; after all, it all fed cash into Hondo's pocket. But recently he'd been a little too ambitious and had been making other contacts, the kind that rang alarm bells for a seasoned businessman like Hondo. Diller seemed to be forming tentative first-step relationships with potential investors and suppliers. Most would recognise this as ambition from a young, very clever man. Most would dismiss it as gallousness. Hondo shared those views but he also saw it for what it was; Diller was manoeuvring himself into a position where a share of the market would eventually be his alone. After that, he'd begin picking away at Hondo's business. Hondo recognised the tactic from business school, all those years ago, and from his own aggressive entrance into the drug business.

With this in mind, he'd knowingly allowed Diller to take more and more Coke, bigger and more expensive shipments on the tic, and now the kid had a choice: pay up, or deal with Wee Hondo. The hundred grand Hondo had demanded was unrealistic in the timescale he'd issued, but not impossible. If he managed it by Friday, Diller would incur a serious dent in his capital and exhaust his supply. It'd set his ambitions back a year or two and in that time, Hondo could work on bringing Diller closer into his circle, maybe salvage his plan to have Diller partner up with Lionel.

If Diller didn't pay up, then despite both the complicated task of 'disappearing' a copper's son and his own personal admiration of the boy, Hondo would have no choice but to act. Either way, Diller would be dealt with.

"Hey Da!" Wee Hondo yelled up from the basement. "It's getting a bit stacked doon here. We need to get some of this cash to Green Billy for laundering."

Big Hondo grinned widely at the image of the full basement in his minds-eye. *Diller first, then Green Billy can get round here and clear this out.*

"Aye, son. I'll sort that out."

Pulling on his leather jacket and grabbing his helmet, Big Hondo headed for the back door. "I'm away for a ride son, see you in an hour."

Slamming the door without waiting for a reply, Hondo mounted his Harley Fat-Boy and gunned the engine, nice and loud, bringing a grin to his face. Heart thumping with the thrill of being the only place he felt truly free, Hondo released the clutch and tore out of his driveway, headed for Eaglesham and a good, long ride. He always thought clearest when riding on his Harley, and in the early hours those country roads would mostly belong to him alone.

Two hours later, as the sun had begun to appear, Hondo roared into Eaglesham. A tiny village on the route between East Kilbride and Ayr, Eaglesham had conservation status, in that it was a lovely village and people wanted it kept that way. Hondo gunned the engine of his Harley loudly as he drove to the last little detached cottage on Moor Road which sat next to the *Leaving Eaglesham* sign. Pulling into the driveway, Hondo gave his Fat-Boy one last rev, bringing a light on in the house and a very pissed-off lady in her dressing gown to the door.

"For fuck sake, James."

"Sorry, hen." Hondo laughed loudly as he dismounted his bike. Grabbing his irate sister in both arms, he lifted her from the ground and planted a wet kiss on her cheek.

"You need a shave," she told him, hiding a smile.

"What's for breakfast, Helen?"

Punching her younger brother in the chest, she told him, "Get in here, yer letting the heat out, James."

After the siblings had filled their stomachs with a full Scot's breakfast of square-sausage, links, black pudding, tattie scone and eggs, they took a mug of tea each into Helen's living room. Taking a seat by the fireplace, Helen sighed as she sank into the familiar curves of her favourite chair.

"Well, Jim. You going to tell me why you're here?"

The big man shifted his arse cheeks around, flattening the over-puffed cushion of the seldom-used chair and buying himself a few seconds.

"Well, eh... It's business, Helen."

Helen started to get out her chair, waving him off. "You've been told before, Jim. I'm no interested in what you call yer business."

Rising to meet her, Hondo placed both hands on her shoulders and guided her gently back into her chair. "Helen, please. I need to talk to you."

Helen regarded her younger brother over the top of her mug as she took a long drink of her sweet tea.

It'd been a long time since she'd seen Jim looking upset about anything.

"Go on then, Jim, but I don't want to hear anything illegal, you hear me?"

Hondo nodded. Retaking his seat, he took a minute or two and the rest of his tea to think about how he could present the Diller problem to Helen without too much detail. He hated coming to his sister, but he didn't have anyone else, and despite already knowing what course of action he was going to take to curb Diller's ambitions, he wanted... well, he supposed he wanted Helen to give him a reason to keep the kid alive. The thought of disposing of Davie Diller was bothering him more than he liked to admit.

Hondo spent the next ten minutes using phrases like *employee, takeover, product, assets, competition* and *eliminate.* Helen nodded along, tutted, rolled her eyes and scowled throughout.

When he'd finished, Helen left the room and returned a few minutes later with more tea and some toast. They sat quietly together drinking and eating whilst Helen, this time, chose her words.

"Why can't you just walk away from this *business*, James? You've made plenty of money over the years. Pack up and go somewhere warm. Walk away."

Hondo sat forward in his chair. "It's not that simple, Helen. I've worked hard to build that business. Young Lionel needs me."

Helen jabbed a finger accusingly at him. "You stop right there, James Crosbie. It's bad enough that you've got our Da sitting in that house... dealing," she spat the word at him, "your filth. You should never have gotten young Lionel involved, look at him now, he's a bloody thug. Why? For your pride, because your anger at being made redundant made you determined to show them all that you still had a purpose, didn't it?"

It wasn't a question. Hondo wanted to argue, but really, what could he say? She was right.

"Well, you've shown everyone what a big man you are, Jim. You've made your money, you've got your respect, and you have nothing left to prove to anyone." Helen stood and took her brother's face in her hands. "No one except me. Oh, God, James, the things you've done... Just cash out, prove to me that my wee brother's still in there somewhere. You were such a sweet kid, such a good husband to Mary."

Hondo rose to his feet at the mention of his late wife, roughly shoving Helen from his path. "Don't start about Mary. It's their fault... them." He jabbed at some unseen enemy out the window, in the past.

"She worried herself sick in the run-up to the steelworks closing. Worries about how we'd feed the family, put clothes on our backs, worried about… about me." Hondo sagged a little at the memory of anyone besides his sister caring about him.

Helen came close to her brother, watched tears well in his eyes and took both of his hands in hers.

"It's time to stop, Jim. Just stop and go away somewhere that no one knows you. Take Lionel and start over again."

For a second or two Helen saw the light of possibility in his eyes. But only for a moment, and then it was replaced by the same iron resolve to always be right, to be in control, to be purposeful, that had been there since Mary went.

"I'm sixty-eight, Helen," Hondo took his hands and turned away from her. Pulling on his jacket and helmet, Hondo opened the front door. "I'm no at the start, hen. I'm at the end."

Hondo shut the door behind him, wishing he'd never come. All he'd done was transfer his doubts and sadness to his sister. He knew what he had to do. Stick with the plan, get Diller on board or, regrets or no, bury the bastard.

His engine rattling every window on Eaglesham Road, his heart swollen and bruised, Hondo headed home.

# TUESDAY

# Chapter 5

## DCI Douglas Diller

Stevie, coffee in each hand and a bag of McMuffins under his arm, shouldered his way through the blue wooden doors into Bellshill police station straight into the path of a young, uniformed PC headed the other way.

"Fur fuck sake son!" Stevie hollered at the young copper as coffee scalded his hand, "that's a coffee ye owe me."

The PC showed a flash of anger before his training took over. "Sir, might I suggest a less aggressive tone when you're addressing a police officer?"

Stevie cocked an eyebrow in amusement and annoyance. Mostly in annoyance. "Never mind yer pish, wee man. Get yer arse down tae McDs and get a large cappuccino for the gaffer."

The PCs wee puffed-out chest deflated a little.

"Gaffer?"

"Aye," Stevie nodded his head, indicating that he should turn around. "That coffee you just assaulted me with was destined for the hand of DCI Douglas Diller."

Stevie gave the kid a moment to turn and acknowledge the appearance of his commanding officer.

"I'd go, PC Whitelaw, before ex-Detective Sergeant Miller sticks a boot up your lazy hole."

PC Whitelaw nodded and made for the car keys behind the desk.

"Never mind, Bawbag," Stevie conceded, "I'll have half a cup. Dougie, here," he offered the full cup to his former colleague, "you have mine." Addressing Whitelaw once more Stevie growled, "Beat it, dick."

Whitelaw looked very much like he wanted to retort, but kept his mouth shut and did as instructed.

"Still not any more fond of probationers, Stevie?" Dougie accepted the full cappuccino.

"I'm not overly fond of any of you pricks these days, Dougie. Where'd you find these wee fannies?" Stevie nodded at the door that Whitelaw had departed through. "He's no' a polis. Can you imagine a laddie like that in the force when we came through? Pffft." He blew a whistle of disapproval through his teeth.

"It's a different world, Stevie," Douglas laughed. "PC Whitelaw has a degree in business and in fannying about with computers. That's the future of the force right there. He'll have my job in about ten years."

Stevie grimaced, scanning Dougie's face for a sign of humour. "Get tae fuck, Dougie. Yer joking?" he asked hopefully.

"'Fraid not, Stevie." Douglas took a sip of his coffee and sat himself down behind the desk.

"Jeezus. One more reason to hate you pricks in blue I suppose." Stevie wasn't really joking, but Dougie laughed anyway to side-step any tension.

"How's tricks then, Stevie?" Douglas asked as he inspected the contents of a sausage and egg McMuffin before deciding not to bother and chucking it back in the grease-marked bag.

"Aye, fine. Look, Dougie, I'm a night worker these days. It doesn't suit me to be up and about before the lunchtime menu at McDonalds, so why don't you just tell me what it is you're wanting?"

Dougie leaned back in his seat, his smile fading. "It's David. My David. I'm a wee bit worried about the company he's keeping."

Stevie filled his mouth with a gulp of coffee to avoid replying. He motioned for Dougie to continue "He's always out, even on a school night. I know that he's not a wean anymore, but he's never in. I heard that he's been hanging about up at Angel's. You see him much?"

Stevie took a bite of his muffin and chewed over his reply along with the grease-slick 'meat'. He hated lying to Dougie. Of all people, loyalty and history meant that he deserved better from Stevie, but Stevie didn't subscribe to those ideals or live in Dougie's world anymore. *Neither did Davie, if he ever did.* As he thought it, the wrap and the money from Dougie's son felt heavier in his coat pocket.

"Look, Dougie. Davie's in a few times a week, but he's hanging about wi' a good crowd. Folk wi' money, they're not scumbags. Actually, they're the professional types. He's no' a big drinker and he doesn't cause any bother. He's just enjoying himself." *And making a fuckin' fortune for himself and Big Hondo.*

Dougie looked a little relieved for a second before his face hardened again.

"What is it Dougie, spit it out."

Stevie was getting impatient. It was all right for Douglas sitting behind his cosy desk, and leaving for a nice comfortable house at dinner time. Stevie had a shift from six pm until three am, standing freezing his bollocks off outside and he was missing out on sleep.

"We had a young guy in here a couple of weeks back," Dougie said. "Picked him up with a couple of grams of coke. Hondo's coke, just cut a wee bit. Personal use, he said. He got a caution and sent home. On the way out the door, the desk sergeant overheard him worrying about repercussions and mentioning somebody called 'Diller'."

"So what?" interrupted Stevie. "It's just some wee druggie worrying about the DCI Diller."

Dougie shook his head. "Naw, Stevie. I'd never met the guy. I had no part in his arrest or processing. Do you think he was talking about Davie?"

"Don't be daft. Davie doesn't hang about wi' folk like that. Look, Dougie, you've nothing to worry about with Davie Diller." *True.* "That boy of yours is a grafter." *True.* "Davie's far too clever to get into trouble wi' folk like this wee guy." *True.* "As for Hondo, what the fuck would a smart guy like Davie be doing anywhere near someone like that?" *Lie.*

Dougie looked a little less worried than he had before. "Davie's always had a wee element of danger about him, y'know?"

"Away tae fuck, Dougie. Just cos yer son likes a bit of risk doesn't mean he's out doing drugs and fuckin' about wi' folk like Hondo. The wee guy was just worrying that the station DCI would get involved. Davie's got nothing to do with this. You know that."

Dougie smiled warmly at Stevie. "Aye, you're right enough. Even if he was the type, he works too hard to have time for that shite. Thanks, Stevie."

"Nae bother DCI. Right, if you're all done being a mother-hen, I'm off."

Without waiting on a reply, Stevie headed for the door. As he approached the exit, PC Whitelaw re-entered with one of the station dogs dragging along behind. Catching scent of the coke wrapped tightly in Stevie's inside jacket pocket, the wee spaniel went ape-shit, barking, yelping and pointing the metaphorical finger at Stevie.

"Seems that Muffin likes you, Ex-Detective Sergeant Miller," PC Whitelaw scowled at Stevie.

"That dug's as big a fuckin' poof as you are, son." Stevie barged past him and out the door.

Whitelaw started after Stevie. "I think you'd better come back here, sir."

"Fuck off, goon," Stevie replied without turning back.

Douglas walked around to the front door and pulled PC Whitelaw by the arm. "That dog needs more training, Whitelaw. His heid's up his arse."

Following the DCI back inside, PC Whitelaw looked unconvinced.

After a hundred yards or so, Stevie fished his iPhone from his pocket and scanned for Davie's number. It was early, so he'd probably be on his way towards the school. As the ring tone started, he heard a phone ringing behind him and turned to see Davie ten feet away.

"Could've just shouted on me, Stevie," Diller laughed.

"Aye, listen." Stevie brushed off the humour. "Dougie's been asking questions about your 'night job'. Nothing serious but I'd make a point of meeting up with yer dad and laying on the charm."

Diller's eyes narrowed as he thought through the possibilities. "That boy Kenzo got picked up the other week. Did he open his mouth?"

*Fuck, this boy is lethally quick* thought Stevie. "Na, nothing deliberate, Davie, the desk-jockey that booked him overheard the name Diller mentioned when Kenzo was being released."

Diller's face was the coldest of steel. "Right. Thanks, Stevie. See you later, it's time for school.

Stevie raked in the McDonalds bag for the last McMuffin, eyeing Davie's back as he headed towards Bellshill Academy. *Aye, Dougie, your boy's far too clever to get himself in the shit* he thought bitterly.

# Chapter 6

## Dad

Diller's mind was working smoothly and calmly on automatic pilot in his first class of the day, sorting through the options for dealing with the Kenzo problem. Everyone around him was scribbling away in silence, heads down. Diller sat in a similar posture, absent-mindedly doodling away on his paper whilst he mulled things over. Kenzo, Kenneth Zolte, was a good wee dealer who'd never previously been collared by the police before. The son of a Polish locksmith, Kenzo was clever, but not too clever, and he had a good array of skills learned from his old man which had proved handy in the past. Kenzo, at twenty-two years old, had also been consistently reliable up until now, a rarity in the business. The choice Diller had was to either issue a warning or to silence him.

It wasn't an ethical choice Diller was working through, merely logistics. Kenzo was a good dealer, for sure, but his right-hand man, Weasel, was just as capable if less bright. Still, that was likely to be a benefit; Weasel could easily take over. Kenzo's team would miss his lock-picks but Diller had always been uneasy with their side-line in burglary. It wouldn't necessarily be a bad thing if the team were less likely to rob houses if they were without Kenzo's assistance.

These considerations all took a distant second to Diller's primary concern. Could Kenzo be trusted? Once this level of minion began making the wrong noises to the wrong people, it normally became a habit. *Aye. Better safe than sorry*, he decided. Kenzo had been too vocal, and worse, his old man had caught wind of it. Diller worked far too hard at preserving his anonymity to allow someone like Kenzo to put him in the shit.

Reclining back into his seat, Diller relaxed now that the decision had been made and began planning Kenzo's *retirement.*

As he had a free period before lunch, Diller followed Stevie's advice and texted his dad to arrange a lunchtime catch-up. Strolling along toward the school's exit, bag over his shoulder, Diller had been pre-occupied looking over his shoulder and had walked straight into Bowie, who'd deliberately placed himself in Diller's path.

Bowie looked him up and down with the usual expression of disdain mixed with superiority. "Leaving early are we, David?" Bowie indicated Diller's jacket.

Bowie knew well enough that Diller was perfectly entitled to sign himself out of school on free periods, but never missed an excuse to pressure his charge. As head of the English department, Bowie had taken a dislike to Diller from day one in the school. Diller's dad had said that Bowie had always been a bit over the top but was a good, consistent teacher and that he should just ignore Bowie when he got pissy.

*That's easier said than done when you've got him on your back all day, every day, Dad.*

Without bothering to answer, Diller squeezed past the department head and made for the door. Bowie's hand darted out and grabbed Diller's upper arm tightly.

"I asked you a question."

Diller spun around, eyes ablaze. "Get yer fuckin' hands aff me, ya baldy auld cunt!" he screamed, glowering at Bowie.

A satisfied, smug grin widened across Bowie's face. Diller composed himself, turned and exited.

"That's going in the book, Diller," Bowie called after him.

*I'll ram that book up your arse,* Diller thought, but kept his mouth shut and his feet moving.

These sorts of encounters with Bowie were the reason Diller hated the man. He seemed to have a natural ability to push all of Diller's buttons and cause him to expose his real self, if only for a second. So far, Bowie had kept his approaches and Diller's reactions private, but the old pit-bull was keeping a record. Diller had no idea what Bowie had in his book and he was getting sick of being poked at by him. *If only Bowie existed in my other life. Dealing with him would be a great deal easier.*

Smiling at the thought of dealing with the old teacher in the same manner in which Kenzo would soon be dispatched brought a wicked smile of amusement to Diller's face.

*Fuck him. I'll deal with him later.*

Lunch with his old man turned out to be surprisingly easy and fun. Dougie didn't ask him anything about Kenzo's remark, just made a few half-hearted digs about the hours he was keeping – *We don't see that much of you just now, David* – and the normal admonishments about working hard at school. Aside from that, he and Dougie sat and laughed about old times and the latest on Uncle Jack, Dougie's 'artist' brother who made Davie look quiet, and other long-forgotten nonsense from Davie's childhood.

"Och, you were a wee shite," Dougie told his son. "Always up to something. Me and your mum are glad you're doing so well these days, son."

Davie shifted in discomfort.

"Aye. Thanks Dad, look I've got to get back to school. Mr Bowie's keeping an eye on me." Davie grinned at his dad who laughed at the mention and memory of Mr Bowie from his own school days.

"Aye, he's an arse of a man, but keep on his good side, David."

Diller promised his dad that he'd make more of an effort to make it to the dinner table and spend more time with him and Mum. As they parted with a hug and a kiss on the cheek, Diller watched his dad walk along toward his office in the cop-shop. He was looking tired these days, his old man. Diller didn't exactly worry about his dad, but from time to time he realised how little time they spent together; how little time they'd ever really spent together. Dad had worked so hard over the years to put drug-dealers away, and here Davie was essentially employing a team of them. It wasn't a prang of conscience on Diller's part, more an amused acknowledgement.

Shrugging off the thought, Diller pulled both of the zips on his coat up to the neck to keep the wind out and headed back to school, and no doubt another friendly encounter with Mr Bowie.

# Chapter 7

## I'm on the Backshift

Walking along Footfield Road, Stevie expelled two jets of grey smoke through his nostrils in annoyance. For the second time that day, he'd been dragged out of his bed at the whim of a man who made him uncomfortable, but whom he was beholden to. *Got to be at work in two bloody hours but at least this time I might get some in return for my time,* Stevie grumbled to himself as he flicked the butt of his cig into the drain and took a sharp right into the house's driveway. Admiring the impressive Harley, sitting on display, clean and proud as he passed, Stevie hammered his fist on the door with what still sounded like a policeman's knock.

Hondo looked annoyed and tired when he opened the door. "Go fuckin' easy on that door, eh?"

Stevie gave him a lop-sided grin but stayed silent.

"Come in then, Stevie," Hondo barked, mumbling away grumpily to himself as he led the ex-cop through to the living room.

Stevie entered the modest four-bedroomed detached house, noting how minimal the place was for a man of Hondo's means. It was a fuckin' tip inside though, having not seen a woman's touch for years. The house smelled of cannabis, engine oil, beer and stale farts. Stevie hardly noticed as the aroma smelled almost identical to his own place. Noticing a large Bowie knife in a glass cabinet, Stevie subconsciously rubbed his leg wound.

Plonking himself into the armchair that Hondo had indicated, he lit another cig, without asking permission, partly to see if Hondo would object, but mostly because he couldn't go five minutes between cigs.

Hondo let him enjoy his first drag before asking, "So, what do I need tae know, Stevie?"

Stevie sat back and returned his attentions to smoking. "Expensive habit these days," he said holding his cig up, "eight pound-odd per packet for the Marlborough Red, Hondo."

Hondo swore and left the room, to return seconds later with a fat envelope which he threw at Stevie. Stevie pocketed the wad and offered a cheery, "Thanks very much, Hondo. Decent of ye."

Hondo stared hard at him, raising his eyebrows to indicate 'start talking, Bawbag'.

Stevie smiled inwardly and continued smoking. "How's the old man?"

"Never mind the fuckin' old man, Stevie. I've no patience for your shite today," Hondo roared.

Stevie placed his palms up, in mock surrender. "Aye, ok Hondo, calm down." It wasn't like Hondo to be quite so volatile. Something was bothering him.

"Right." Hondo sat back into his chair and regained his composure. "What's the story with young Diller then?"

Stevie didn't mince his words this time. "Davie's in Angel's three or four times a week, dealing directly with the University and professional beaks that come in. He's doing a good bit of business."

Hondo looked irritated again. "Aye, good. What about the other stuff?" Hondo jabbed a finger at Stevie for emphasis.

Stevie lit another cig and continued. "Davie's got about ten wee Neds that I know of dealing for him all over town. He's got that Tawttie over at Skid-Row, Kenzo down the North Road, but that might be changing. I'll come back to him in a minute."

Stevie took a few more drags on his Marlborough whilst he jogged his memory on the names of the rest of Davie's team.

"There's Weasel who works with Kenzo, Big Simmy in the West End, that boy, Spammy, in the Jewel-Scheme…"

"For fuck sake!" Hondo interrupted. "He's not shy is he?"

Stevie shook his head. "He's cutting down some product, meting it out to the Neds and keeping the good stuff for his pals in Angel's. The boy's been throwing it around a bit these last few months, but between his wee Ned crew and his Angel's crowd, Davie's selling more than enough to offset what he's giving away."

Hondo stroked his big moustache thoughtfully. "Aye, he's bringing plenty money in my door, I can't fault him for that, it's the other stuff. You heard anything about Diller meeting with Chubbs Valenti?"

"Chubbs? Naw. Not that I know of, Hondo."

"Well he has. Diller and that pseudo-Italian cunt are setting up their own side-business. A couple of my boys have spotted Diller in Valenti's place a few times when they've been running money over to Green Billy's for me. He's in the same estate."

"You're sure?" Stevie asked. "Just because he's been seen with Chubbs doesn't mean that they're working together."

"As sure as I can be in this game, Stevie. Between that, and his other ambitions, Diller needs to be reigned-in or gotten rid of. I might need some help."

Stevie stayed quiet for a few moments and let Hondo's words sink in. It was one thing to turn a blind eye to Davie's carry-on, even lie about it to Dougie. Christ, he was more than happy to take

Hondo's cash in return for keeping an eye on Diller. What Hondo was talking about now, though, that was different. Was this really what he'd become? He scanned Hondo's face, thinking of the man he used to be and of what Hondo had been to *that* man. Not a friend, that was damn sure.

Stevie had known Davie Diller from birth, had spent family Christmases with the Dillers, shared good times and bad with Dougie. Dougie had done his best to help him after he was stabbed and fell apart mentally. *He hadn't helped in the end though, had he?* Davie was a bit of a player, but as far as Stevie knew, he'd never hurt anyone directly. Could he really put money before the boy's safety?

After chain-lighting his next cig, Stevie planted his feet on Hondo's coffee table and told him, "Count me in."

# Chapter 8

## The Kenzo (Final) Solution

"Thanks for dinner, Mum. I'm off out," Diller shouted from the hall as he opened the front door to exit.

"Just you hang on a minute, David Diller." Maggie Diller sped through from the living room as quickly as her slippers allowed and reached up to catch her son in a tight embrace. "It's been nice to have some family time, David. I don't remember the last time we sat around the table together before today." She released him.

Standing straight again, Davie pulled his coat on. "Aye, I know, Mum. Look, I'll make sure we see each other at breakfast tomorrow morning, how about that?"

Maggie smiled at him, nodding. "Have good night, son. Be careful."

"Aye, Mum. See you then," Davie replied over his shoulder as he went out into what had become an unseasonably frosty evening.

Leaving the house, Diller pushed his hands through the makeshift glove sockets that Superdry coats sometimes had at the cuffs and thought to himself, *That was actually really nice tonight. I will make it to breakfast with Mum.* As Davie rounded the corner onto Hamilton Road his thoughts turned as cold as the night. He increased his pace and headed for Kenzo's place.

School had been a trial that afternoon and he was glad to be out in the nippy evening air with purpose. As he'd expected, Bowie had been on him as soon as he'd re-entered the school building. He'd had a 'chat' with Diller about timekeeping, responsibility, workload and commitments, all the usual, the whole time prodding a fat index finger into Diller's chest to punctuate each remark. "It's just not on, David." *Prod*, "We expect better from someone of your intellect." *Prod.* Diller had stood and borne it, taking his mind and his anger elsewhere – to tonight when he'd share his frustrations with Kenzo.

Several hours later, Diller stood in the darkness beneath a sycamore tree, warming his hands and gently shuffling his feet around to get the blood flowing back in to warm them. He'd been following Kenzo around for most of the evening, watching him from beneath the same tree for the last ninety minutes. Kenzo had been with three of his wee pals drinking, smoking weed and generally loafing around at the entrance to Strathclyde Park from The Glen.

Sitting in the kids' swing park, drinking a bottle of White Lightning and tossing stones at the golf course fence, Kenzo had been on his own for the last half an hour. Diller was getting tired of waiting for him to move somewhere less open and huffed some warm air into his hands in exasperation. Glancing over to his right, he spotted the picnic table that he and Stacey had used for their encounter the previous night. The memory warmed him more thoroughly than any amount of feet-stamping or hand-blowing. *It had been a damn sight milder last night*, Diller reflected.

Diller was tired of waiting.

Fishing an almost-empty Buckfast bottle out of a nearby bush, Diller affected drunkenness and staggered out to greet Kenzo.

"Awright, Kenzo mate," he spat out whilst he made his limbs and body stagger and sway. His eyes watched Kenzo carefully from the darkness under his hood.

Kenzo had turned around, instantly alert, and stiffened further on identifying Diller. Finally Kenzo relaxed when he saw the 'state' that Diller was in. Smiling a predator's smile, he puffed himself up and made his way over to Diller. Clearly thinking Diller-the-drunk to be in no fit state to defend himself, he began pressuring, goading him.

"On yer own, are ye? Ye got any gear? Any cash?"

Kenzo leaned into Diller as he spoke, shouldering him with implied threat. It was one of those innocuous movements that cowards use to threaten which could be shrugged off as nothing should Diller be more sober than he appeared and the need to back off arose.

Diller moved with the push, affecting incoherence and vulnerability.

"Eh? Aye," he slurred. "I've got a stash hidden…" Diller jerked around, as though getting his bearings. Pointing into the forest, he finished, "Over there."

In the short walk towards the thickest part of the forest, Diller allowed Kenzo to insult him a few times and relieve him of his Buckfast. Ignorant of who had discarded the bottle where he'd discovered it, Diller fought off the notion to grin at the thought of where the dark green bottle had been, or what exactly Kenzo was greedily draining from it.

"How much further?" Kenzo demanded after a few minutes of crunching deep into the forest.

"It's just round here," Diller replied sluggishly.

Selecting a massive oak tree, Diller pointed towards the base of its trunk. "Buried it about a foot down, at the bottom ay that tree."

Diller fell on his backside into the humus and detritus of the forest floor and stayed there, looking confused. A glaze of greed and badness slid over Kenzo's eyes.

The look told Diller that once the guy had finished recovering the 'stash', he intended to take advantage of the drunken state Diller was in and give him a beating at the very least.

As Kenzo crouched to big digging, Diller rose steadily and silently to his feet, all pretence gone. Feeling the clarity that only ever came to him at moments when he was truly free to be who… what he was, Diller covered the ground between him and Kenzo in an instant; heart racing, veins swelling, breath bated in anticipation at what was coming.

In one brutally violent lunge, Diller smashed Kenzo's face into the trunk of the massive tree, enjoying the sickening crunch of bark, teeth and bone. He smelled the salty iron of blood in the air and saw the heat-fog rise into the cold air from a gash on Kenzo's skull.

Rolling the unconscious man over, Diller sat on his chest, placed a knee on each of his arms to pin him, and slipped his combat knife out from its hiding place. Pressing the wickedly sharp edge of the blade against the side of Kenzo's throat, Diller produced a smaller blade, also viciously sharp, from somewhere else. With the hand that held the smaller of the blades, Diller made a fist, knuckle-side to Kenzo, and thumped the side of his head to wake him up.

"What the fu…" Kenzo groggily realised the position he was in.

"Shut the fuck up," Diller hissed, quiet as a whisper, allowing spit to fall on Kenzo's face.

*Funny how a bit of drool puts fear into them*, Diller observed with amusement. He was having tremendous fun, no doubt about it, and feeling calmer, more in control, than he had in weeks.

Kenzo went rigid with fear and then, slowly, his eyes changed. Kenzo didn't really believe that any real harm could come to him at Diller's hands. They'd known each other for a while; Diller was a clever guy, a good guy, despite his dealing. It was Diller's way of making him fear him, of keeping him in line. He'd show Diller the respect he deserved, apologise, that would fix it. He'd been stupid, but he could make amends.

Kenzo thought all of these things as he lay with one knife to his throat and the other pressed to the lower eyelid of his right eye.

Diller almost laughed out loud with recognition as he watched the man underneath him go through the stages of denial, trying to convince himself that he was safe. *They all do that too; easier than accepting that they're going to fuckin' die.*

Diller moved his right hand, the hand with the larger blade, away from Kenzo's neck by half an inch.

Kenzo took it as a sign to start talking.

"I'm sorry Davie. I'm pished, mate, I've been a right wanker."

Without a word, Diller moved his blade around and behind Kenzo's neck and slid it through skin, fat, muscle and blood vessel. He felt the blade reach bone and angled the blade ever so slightly down until he felt it slide between two cervical vertebrae and then pulled the knife towards himself until the spongy feel of spinal cord broke and Kenzo stopped screaming. He'd stopped screaming because he felt no more pain from the neck, down. He'd be feeling plenty pain from the neck up, soon enough.

Without the power to move any of his limbs, there was no reason for Diller to maintain his position on top of Kenzo's chest. As he stood, Diller watched with a detached curiosity as Kenzo began to go into shock and convulse; well, as much as a head could convulse on its own. The rest of his body wasn't budging.

"You can't..." Kenzo choked out the words through blood that'd entered his trachea. *Must've cut a little deep*, Diller noted as he watched his victim spray-cough blood and heat-fog into the cold night air. *Ah well. It's a learning process. Better get on with it.*

As Diller walked slowly around Kenzo, choosing his spot, Kenzo spluttered at him, "I've a wee boy. Please don't."

Kneeling beside Kenzo's head, Diller placed a hand behind his neck and lifted it slightly, tilting his head and allowing Kenzo a little more air.

Cocking his own head to the side, Diller spoke softly, sympathetically, to the prone Kenzo.

"This the wee three-year-old laddie? Josh, is it?" Diller asked gently.

Between coughs and splutters and with renewed hope rushing back into his eyes, Kenzo managed to choke out, "Yes."

"It's painful for a kid to grow up without a father, isn't it?" Diller asked softly, deliberately flooding his voice with empathy. "The worst pain, some might say."

"Yes," croaked Kenzo, "yes."

Diller sat back onto his feet. "This the same Josh that you don't bother your arse with? The one who never sees a penny from you? The same Josh that hasn't had a visit, or probably a spare thought, from you in months? The Josh whose teenage mum you kicked the shite out of for months before she got you sent to prison? Is that him? Is that the Josh who needs you?" Diller's voice was calm and gentle as a priest's at a funeral.

Diller watched the tears and the terror rise in Kenzo's eyes and then pushed his small blade, through the eyelid, under the eye and prised upwards until the eyeball slipped loose from its former home. Diller laughed as hard as Kenzo screamed and proceeded to show Kenzo what pain really was.

# WEDNESDAY

# Chapter 9

## Davie Diller's Day Off

"Yes, I won't be into school today, Miss Davidson. That's right, stomach flu. I'm sure I'll be fine by tomorrow. Thanks, Miss Davidson."

Diller pressed the disconnect button and threw his phone onto the sofa. School was most definitely not happening for Diller today. He was in too good a mood following the previous night's adventure and wasn't about to let a Bowie encounter burst his bubble. Besides, he had business to take care of in Kenzo's absence.

Arriving cheerily in Mum's kitchen this morning, he'd consumed a massive breakfast, many times his usual portion size. His ravenous hunger was partly for show to make his mum happy – she was a feeder – but mostly due to the overwhelming sense of vigour he felt. The afterglow of moments like last night didn't last long and Diller didn't intend to waste this one sitting in a classroom. Strolling from the living room back to the kitchen, Diller buttered himself another slice of toast, thanked his mum for breakfast, and headed out for the day.

It was a beautiful morning and Diller had decided to take advantage of the weather by walking to the North Road, rather than taking the bus. After spending an hour or so sorting out Kenzo's little corner of the business, assigning Weasel as top man and dropping off some product as well as a wee incentive to him in the form of a few hundred quid, Diller left them to it. No doubt they'd be wondering where their former leader was, but it'd do them good to be a little more nervous than they'd been recently. Maybe the team would be less likely to end up getting arrested.

Spending the remainder of the morning visiting the rest of his team, Diller enjoyed the sun on his face as he strolled unhurriedly from one part of town to another, stopping for a coffee in Tesco as he passed. By the time Diller had met with Tawttie he'd decided to visit his old man for lunch again at the police station nearby.

As he entered through the station's double doors, a little spaniel appeared from nowhere and started going nuts. Diller resisted the urge to kick it in the ribs and painted an amused grin on his face which was only partially fake. Raising his hands in mock surrender, he told the tiny dog, "I give up, Killer. You've got me."

Diller noticed that his dad had come through from the back office and was having a good laugh at the wee dog terrorising his son.

"Dad," Diller pointed at the little dog, "give me a hand, eh?"

Dougie roared into the office, "Whitelaw! That daft dog of yours is trying to maul this guy out here. Get it tae fuck."

Arrogance and annoyance emanated from PC Whitelaw as he made his way through to the front of the station, leash in hand. Scowling at Davie, he asked, "What's in yer pockets?"

Diller scanned him up and down.

"Yer wife's knickers, *Cunt*-stable. They're fuckin' rotten. No wonder yer dog's going mental." Diller's face was poker-straight; Dougie's was creased with laughter. Whitelaw's wasn't.

"I'll have to ask you to…" Whitelaw began before being interrupted by Dougie.

"Chase yerself, Whitelaw, and train that fuckin' dog properly." Dougie was still laughing.

Whitelaw reddened. "But, Sir..."

"But, nothing Constable." DCI Diller's suddenly severe facial expression left his PC in no doubt that the he no longer found the situation amusing. "Shift yer arse." Dougie jabbed his thumb behind him towards the back office.

Diller bristled with annoyance in reaction to the PC's attitude, but brushed it off, flashing his dad a toothy smile. "What a banger he is, Dad."

"Aye, his dog's a wanker as well." Dougie smiled conspiratorially. "What can I do for you, son?" Dougie punched Davie on the shoulder to punctuate.

"Thought we could go for lunch again, you up for it?"

Dougie shook his head. "Love to, but I can't today. We're pretty busy in here at the minute and not just keeping that daft dug from ripping the baws off innocent members of the public."

Diller's ears practically pricked up.

"Busy, eh? Anything juicy?"

Dougie smiled. "Nothing major, son, a missing person and some shifting amongst the druggie crowd. Nothing you'd be interested in. Just some lowlife called Kenzo."

Diller felt his dad scan him with a Detective Chief Inspector's gaze, gauging his reaction.

*Somebody's noticed Kenzo's absence already,* Diller thought. *It's obviously still annoying Dad that my name was mentioned.* It was unsettling to have Dad looking at him this way, but Diller had had more than enough practice at hiding the truth, even from a walking lie detector like DCI Diller. Hiding any signs of recognition from his face was second nature, an automatic response.

Diller casually dunked into his pocket for a pack of Polo-mints, offered one to his dad, and popped another into his mouth. "Where do these guys get their names from? Kenzo, for fuck sake?"

DCI Diller stared for a second longer, taking in Davie's nonchalance, and then suddenly his face broke into a smile. "Watch the language... Baw-bag." He grinned at Davie.

Diller laughed at his father's joke and at his own skill in deception. It was so easy. People convinced themselves that they were mistaken when confronted with things they didn't want to be true.

"Better get back to school then, Da."

Reaching over the wide desk, Diller punched Dougie on the upper arm, and headed quickly for the exit.

"See ye, son," Dougie said quietly, sad-faced, as Davie disappeared through the door.

Diller turned left as he walked away from the police station and headed along past Morrisons towards the Cultural Centre, rather than to Bellshill Academy. Feeling fairly carefree, he kicked an empty Coke can along the pavement as he strolled.

Had he been paying more attention, he might've noticed the Transit van with whited-out rear windows cruising along the road behind him. He might've heard the two massive men lunging towards him from behind. He didn't. Instead he punched and kicked and bit ferociously but futilely as the men pulled a thick bag over his head, then dragged him to and threw him into the waiting van. He did hear the doors slam, feel the thud of the van's floor against his face and the weight of one of the men holding him and the other tying him. The last thing he felt was the blow to his head.

Lights flashed, brightening the inside of Diller's eyelids, as he slowly regained consciousness. Keeping his eyes closed and his body still he used his ears, trying not to tilt his head, to follow sounds to determine where the hell he was. The place echoed metallically with each footstep around him. Three distinct voices added to the effect. Moving his right foot, leg and left hand an imperceptible amount, Diller noted that his hands and feet were tied to a wooden structure, probably a chair as he was sitting upright. His foot scratched at debris on the floor; the smell of metal and industry was everywhere. It smelled entirely familiar.

As the voices sounded a distance away he chanced a slow raise of an eyelid for a second and recognised the building immediately: the steelworks. More specifically, he'd awoken in an abandoned section of the mostly closed-down works. Diller had played here as a child with his cousins. Running, climbing, fighting and destroying the remaining fixtures and fittings, the boys had made the leftover industrial shell their own private, rusted playground. He knew the building well and felt comforted by its familiarity, despite his current circumstances.

Diller had made his first cut in human skin in this building. As cousins do, he and his older cousin, Paul, had formed a pact here, Diller cutting Paul's hand as well as his own with a scrap of metal after Paul had been unable to cut himself. They'd vowed to be inseparable, blood brothers for life and had been taken for a tetanus vaccination after Paul's mum had spotted the cuts.

Paul's life had ended one year later when he died from leukaemia, holding his blood brother's hand, scars pressed tightly together. None of the adults had wanted Davie to be there, saying it was no place for a ten year old. Diller recalled thinking at the time, *Paul's ten and he has to be here.* The two cousins had screamed and begged and demanded to be allowed that time together and eventually the adults capitulated. In the end Davie spent days at Paul's bedside watching him waste and suffer and die. He simply wouldn't be moved, not by anyone. Uncle Cameron had quickly emigrated to New Zealand with the rest of the family after Paul's death.

Sensing that the men in the room had grown quiet, Diller shook off the memories. He assumed that the sudden silence was probably in deference to the man he'd just heard arrive on a loud Harley. The man who'd arranged his new accommodation was also a man who was even more familiar with the steelworks than Diller himself was.

Giving up the pretence of sleep, Diller kept his chin low and looked up into the inch-away face of Big Hondo.

"Nice to see you Hondo," Diller smiled up at him, cocking an eyebrow.

"Always a pleasure, Davie," Hondo replied, a little sadly, pulling another chair over to sit more or less level with Diller.

Diller had expected Hondo to be raging at him, threatening him at the very least, but he just sat there, looking sadly across at him like a disappointed parent who'd caught his offspring up to no good. Diller didn't like the pity he saw. It angered him, but he forced the anger down and nonchalance into his voice.

"Cup ay tea would be nice."

Hondo battered his cheek with a heavy back-hander.

"Don't," he told Diller. "You're here to listen. Understand?"

Diller spat a mouthful of fresh blood onto Hondo's cowboy boots, earning himself another backhander, a heavier one this time.

"There's nae point in talking to him, Da." Wee Hondo strolled in through the open double doors and over to where his dad and Diller sat. "Let me take over."

Big Hondo, still seated, turned his attention back to Diller. "Is that what you want? Is it, Davie?"

Diller ignored the question. Flicking his eyes up and across to Wee Hondo, Diller allowed a massive grin of excitement to light up his face. "Lionel!" He sounded so happy to see the guy. "You're putting the beef on, big man."

Laughing at his own remark, Diller turned his attention back to Big Hondo, who was shaking his head and rising from his chair.

Grabbing Diller roughly by the back of his head, Big Hondo forced Diller to make eye contact with him. "You're a cocky wee bastard, Davie. I should put a knife in you."

Diller could see that Hondo wanted him to be scared, he needed him to be. It would let Hondo know that there was perhaps a chance that Diller still had sense enough to get back in line. All Hondo saw in

Diller's blue eyes was disinterest and a mocking, mild amusement. He released him and took a few steps away. Stopping in front of his son, Hondo placed a hand on his shoulder, and kept his back to Diller whilst he addressed him.

"I want my money, so you've still got 'til Friday. Wee Hondo here will give you a wee something to motivate ye." Hondo squeezed his son's shoulder. "Don't get carried away, Lionel. Just a wee minding for the boy."

For the next thirty minutes following Hondo's departure, Lionel did his very best to make Diller scream. Removing four of his finger nails with pliers, sliding the nails as slowly as he could manage, Lionel waited patiently for him to crack, to show him something.

As he searched for something to savour, all he found in Diller's eyes was defiance, hatred and the promise of retribution. Diller sat impassive, internalising the pain, storing it away for a time when he would repay every last moment, every scream of a neuron, with interest.

Diller knew pain intimately. Paul's final days and his death had taught him everything about emotional and physical pain, and helplessness and horror. It had taught him that some people can take pain and some can't. Paul couldn't take it. His eyes had pleaded and begged Diller for hours to help him. Nothing did help him; not the morphine, not the doctor's promises, not his parent's prayers and not the priest's words. Paul suffered, truly suffered, until Davie finally used the pillow to give his blood brother his peace.

Paul couldn't take pain, but some people can. Some people can take it because deep down, somewhere even they themselves can't feel it, they hate themselves and they use that hate to absorb pain others would find unbearable. Deep down they know that they deserve it and all that their tormentor is doing is giving them back pain that's already theirs, returning pain they already own. Deep down they know that they deserve to suffer.

They analyse the pain that arrives, feel it and bring it into themselves, using it for strength. Pain was Paul's legacy to him; the only times Diller felt truly alive was with pain as his companion. It didn't matter whether the pain was his or someone else's.

Diller watched detachedly as Lionel pulled the fourth nail from his fingertip. Silently he promised Wee Hondo that he'd teach him all about real pain. Soon.

# Chapter 10

## A Useless Five-Percent-er

Stevie removed his leather bomber jacket and threw it onto the ram-raid post to his left. *Bloody warm tonight.*

Having to wrestle two deadbeats out of Angel's hadn't helped him in staying cool either.

"Haw, Monkey," he bellowed.

One of Stevie's co-workers, a temp who had been hired from Rock Steady for the night, looked up at him. When temps appeared to provide an extra pair of hands on busy nights, Stevie didn't bother to learn their names, but gave them nicknames based on their face or mannerisms. In the last few months, he'd worked with Mongers, Budgie, Nicki Minaj, Posh Spice and Django. Tonight's guy was a bit simian-looking so had been christened, Monkey. Around an hour into his shift, Monkey had given up trying to tell Stevie his name, figuring that it was less trouble to simply answer to his new moniker.

"Aye?" Monkey asked.

"I'm going to stretch my legs and have a cig. You take over here Monkey-Boy."

Stevie loped off, lighting a Marlborough as he went. Hearing his colleague huffing, he tossed over his shoulder. "I'll bring ye a nice banana back."

Monkey jabbed his middle finger at Stevie's back as he left.

Half an hour later, Stevie was in a dark corner on the perimeter of the Tunnock's factory. Leaning back against the brick, Stevie inhaled deeply on a Marlborough and craned his neck back to stare up at the sky, trying to enjoy the moment. All of his senses were sharpened but not in a good way. His nerves were shredded, every sound irritated him. The cold scratchy bricks on his bare arse cheeks chafed and Linda's teeth, rather than stoking his lust as they gently nibbled and dragged back and forth assisting her lips, well, they just hurt. His semi had all but wilted to a five percent insult of an erection despite Linda's finest efforts to revive it.

"Stop, hen, just stop there," Stevie told her.

"What's the matter, Stevie?" Linda looked up at him.

"Och, I've a lot on my mind, hen."

"We could try something else?" Linda took a step to the wall, braced both hands on the brickwork and rotated her pelvis, presenting her peach of an arse to Stevie.

Stevie laughed, causing her to self-consciously straighten and cover herself over with her coat.

"Don't ye fancy me anymore?" she accused him, looking ten percent hurt, ninety percent pissed-off.

"Och, it's not you, it's me, Linda," Stevie offered, standing pathetically covering himself while his trousers lay around his ankles.

Linda poked a finger in his face. "Did you just say that? To me?" she screamed at him, overdramatically.

"I didn't mean it like that, hen. I've really not been right." Stevie had his palms open in a submissive gesture.

"Aye, well," Linda told him, lighting a cigarette. "I've not got time for this. Gies a phone when it's working again." She jabbed a finger down at his crotch and departed, wobbling away on her fantastic legs and too-high heels.

Stevie sighed and lit another Marlborough. Holding the cig in his mouth he tucked away his soggy wee pal and did up his trousers. He'd been struggling badly to focus since he'd met with Hondo the previous day. Hardly sleeping at all the previous night, Stevie had tossed and turned, trying to figure out who and what he'd become. Had he really promised Hondo that he would *help* with Davie Diller?

Since he'd left the force, Stevie's life had gone to shit. He'd lost and thrown away everything good in his life. The job, the house, his wife, their daughter; in an eighteen-month spell he'd lost the lot. Looking back, it was clear that in the months following his medical retirement Stevie had been badly depressed and in the darkest depths of PTSD. That one split second when the knife had slid into his thigh had changed his life forever and continued to define his actions now.

\*\*\*\*\*\*\*\*\*\*

DS Miller had been standing bullshitting about football with the boy behind the desk in the Shell petrol station when the call came in. An informant of his had tipped him off a few days previously that a substantial deal was taking place in The Orb, and that Hondo would be there in person, holding product. The call informed him that the deal was on.

DS Miller contacted the station, looking for the DCI to get the go-ahead, but Dougie was still down at Wishaw General visiting that nephew of his, the laddie with leukaemia. That meant that it was the Sergeant's call. Relaying orders for a few uniformed officers to liaise with him on Hamilton Road, DS Miller went directly there on foot. Accepting a stab-proof vest from the attending DC, DS Miller briefed each of the half dozen officers, instructing them to go for Hondo first and then arrest any stragglers.

Almost as soon as the team burst through the door of The Orb bar, DS Miller spotted Hondo holding court at the far end of the bar. Team-handed they dragged him and three of his cronies to the sticky floor, cuffed and searched him. Nothing.

Hondo laughed at them throughout. "Better luck next time," the old man had sneered at DS Miller as he was released from the barely-on cuffs.

"Just wait the now," Miller told his team.

Stepping outside, he radioed the station. Five minutes later the dog team arrived. The station dog, a massive German Shepard named Kaiser, sniffed from man to man, finding nothing. The handler proceeded to lead Kaiser around the pub whilst Hondo and his crew laughed to themselves. Suddenly the mutt had leapt over the bar and begun scratching and barking at the cellar door.

"If there's nothing else Sergeant? "Hondo laughed and left the pub. DS Miller had no excuse to stop him leaving.

Opening the cellar door, Miller had shouted down into the darkness, "Up ye come." Suddenly a man flashed through the open hatch. Bowie knife in hand, the suspect had plunged the eight-inch blade into

Miller's leg and ended his career in a spray of blood and violence.

When he'd still been on active duty, Stevie had scoffed at other officers who had succumbed to PTSD after an incident on duty. *If they can't cope wi' the job, they should fuck off out of it* had been his assertion.

Like most officers he'd worked with, Stevie had considered mental illness a preventable and controllable condition. *Just cheer up. Just don't think about it. Just work harder*.

Now he knew better. Stevie had spent hours crying for no reason. He'd slept for days at a time, starved himself and ignored everyone. He'd tried to re-engage but couldn't face the simple act of talking to another person. Hell, he couldn't even look at his own wife without suffering a panic attack. His daughter had cried at him, begging him to pull himself together. *Don't you love us anymore, Dad?* It had broken his heart. Inside he was screaming "Yes! Help me!'" Outside, he rolled over and went to sleep whilst his broken-hearted family packed their things and left him.

He drank and did drugs. He gambled, and then, finally, eventually, he faced the world again. The doc had given him pills that helped him to face people, but the guy who emerged through the black fog with a medicine cabinet full of anti-depressants at home and a bloodstream full of whiskey and Class-As wasn't really Stevie Miller anymore. He just wore him like a suit.

Who he was now – no family, reeking of cigarettes, alcohol and bitterness – would have sickened DS Miller. But he was who he was. He didn't know how to be his old self anymore. The guy who'd laughed freely with people, who'd spent all of his free time with his family. The guy who people knew would do what he said he would and could be relied upon to back you up. The husband, the father and the police officer were all long gone and all that remained, it seemed, was the piece of shit, alcoholic, coke-snorting doorman who'd sell out his best friend's son for the favour of a petty local drug dealer.

The old DS Miller would have detested Stevie Miller, but not half as much as he hated himself. Just like his dick, he was about five percent of what he should be.

*Fuck it.* Stevie tossed the butt of his cigarette at the wall. *Five percent's better than fuck all. Hondo can go fuck himself. Young Davie was a bit of a player but that could be sorted. Davie had never hurt a soul. He didn't deserve what was coming to him.*

Stevie straightened himself and headed back to Angel's to finish his shift.

# Chapter 11

## Michael Jackson and Bubbles

Hunched over, hands deep inside the sleeves of his coat for protection, Diller slipped through the school gates and made his way around to the back of the building. Kicking the door to save him using his hands to knock, Diller sighed with relief as Stacey opened the rear door for him. He didn't know Cardinal Newman High School very well, but Stacey's instructions had been clear.

"Davie, what's happened to you?" Stacey had spotted the burst nose and bruising that had already formed on his face.

Diller slipped his hands through his jacket sleeves, and held them up for her to see.

"Oh God, Davie. Get in here."

Stacey led him to the school's little first-aid room and clattered around in cupboards and drawers for a minute or so collecting liquids, cotton wool and bandages.

"Sit here," she told him. Pushing his hands into a metal bowl filed with antiseptic, she waited for him to wince but saw no reaction.

"You're not going to tell me what happened, are you?"

Diller shook his head. "I can't, Stace." He wiggled his fingers in the bowl silently for a second or two, enjoying the clarity of the sting.

Stacey reached out and touched his cheek in the one place that looked like it wouldn't hurt. "Come on. Let's get this cleaned up."

Carefully treating each of his nail-less fingertips, the cuts on his nose and cheek, Stacey then began applying ointment and bandages to each of his fingers. Davie stood up. "Just plasters on the fingertips please, Stacey. I need to use my hands."

"You need to keep these clean, Davie. I'm using bandages. Band-Aids are no good."

Diller held her hand lightly. "Please, Stacey, just the plasters."

Looking miffed, Stacey did as he asked despite her annoyance. Retrieving a big box marked 'Multi-coloured Band-Aids', she proceeded to place a different coloured plaster on each of his damaged fingertips. "Blue, pink, yellow and purple. There ye go, tough-guy. MJ lives."

Diller did a short Moonwalk in reply, making her laugh.

"Seriously, Davie, you should go to the hospital."

Ignoring her remark, Diller put his arms around her and pulled her in close. "Thank you."

Shrugging him off, Stacey told him, "Don't be getting all lovey with me, son. Friends with benefits, that's what we agreed." She was grinning.

"Aye, and some benefits they are," Diller laughed.

"You had better be going home, Davie?"

An icy-seriousness slid over Diller's face. "Na. I've got people to meet at Angel's."

Stacey shook her head. "Go on then. Off ye go."

Diller turned to leave but halted as Stacey took a firm grasp of his forearm.

"Hang on a minute, Davie."

Diller sat back down, nodding his head in a gesture that conveyed, *go on then*. Stacey sighed and sat next to him, taking him by the arms again, avoiding his hands.

Staring out the little window in her office, she looked sad for a moment before talking.

"Do you remember ma mum, Davie?"

He did. She'd been a big MILF in her younger years, and in all honesty Davie would probably still fire into her, just for the novelty; she was a good looking woman.

"Aye," he said.

"Well, you'll remember the state she used to get into, with the drink... and the drugs?" Stacey looked into his eyes, her own quivering and misting a little as she dredged up rusted memories that were perhaps better left lying to rot.

"Aye," Diller said softly. "I remember."

Stacey shifted her damp eyes back to the widow, giving Diller her profile.

"One Christmas, Mum bought me this bike; my first bike. I was probably five years old. It was beautiful." She smiled at the memory for a second and then turned stone-faced. "I played with it all day long on Christmas day, this beautiful pink bike, with tassels on the handles and clean, white pedals. I loved it. Mum made me stay in the house with it. We had a long hallway, so I didn't mind... not really." She smiled sadly at the thought of herself happily coasting up and down the hall.

"I went to bed happier than I could ever remember being. I felt surrounded by love that night; that was a rare feeling for me then, in those days. I thought that only someone who really, really loved you could put such thought into finding such a perfect present for you. That's what I fell asleep thinking: how loved I was." Stacey smiled again, a sadder smile this time.

"When I woke up the next morning, the pedals were off of my bike. I asked Mum why and she told me that the bike, my bike, was faulty and that she'd send it back to the catalogue the next day for a better one, one that wasn't broken. It would be back in a few days, she promised. I watched her take my beautiful bike away and planked myself on the window sill. Remember those big windows in the flat?"

Diller nodded.

"Well, I sat there every day at eleven o'clock, when the post came, waiting for my new bike to come. I sat there every day, Davie. Day after day, she'd tell me, *I'm sure that it'll be here tomorrow, hen. Just wait and see.* After six months I finally figured out that she'd sent it back and gotten a refund for money for drink."

Stacey turned back to look into Diller's eyes. Hers were no longer moist, they were steel.

"I got that bike for one day and spent dozens of days afterwards deluded, waiting desperately for it to come back. Who does that to their children, Davie?"

"I know, Stace. It's shite." Diller put a hand over hers, the one that still rested on his arm. He didn't like this kind of closeness with anyone; it reminded him of holding Paul's hand. *No don't go there.*

Stacey shrugged him off and took his face in both of her hands. "That's what you're like, Davie. You give a little of yourself and you take it away before anyone can love it too much. You're a fucking Indian Giver with your affection." Stacey laughed at this, then turned serious again. "You need to sort yourself out, Davie."

Diller looked away from her piercing eyes. "I thought you were happy with a wee shag now and again, Stacey."

She burst out laughing. "I don't want to marry you, ya arsehole; I want you to let me be your friend."

She reached out to his face again and rested her palm against his cheek. "You need to let somebody love you, Davie... as a friend."

Diller stood up from the table they'd been sitting on and pulled his zips up tight, closing his coat.

"Wouldn't know how. I'll see ye later, hen."

"Go on then." Stacey nodded at the door and watched him leave.

Diller ingested some paracetamol and ibuprofen and snorted a thin line of Charlie to help him along and then headed straight to Angel's. Hopping out of his taxi at the front of the bar, Diller noticed that Stevie wasn't around. *Must have taken a break.* Thinking that he was unlikely to run into any of Hondo's men again today after the friendly reminder he'd had earlier, he strolled towards the pub. The doorman shoved a palm straight into Diller's path as he approached the door.

"Where you going, mate?" the guy asked him.

Diller had to laugh out loud. *What a fuckin' day.*

"I'm going in there, what's it look like? Where's Stevie? He'll keep ye right."

Diller moved to enter the pub and found the guy's hand on his chest. "Do you not think that maybe you're the wrong age group to be in here?" the guy asked him.

For the first time in a long while, Diller was actually speechless and stood staring dumbly at the doorman for a full second.

"Look, mate," he told the guy, "get out ma fuckin' way."

The doorman placed himself, arms folded, in Diller's path. "Ye've been told, Michael Jackson," he nodded at Diller's plasters, "ye can fuck off somewhere else."

Diller couldn't actually get angry at the guy, he was too pathetic. "Michael Jackson is it? That must make you Bubbles then, ya monkey-looking prick."

A resigned look crossed Monkey's face as he looked over Diller and saw Stevie coming. Clearly Stevie had heard the exchange.

"Get tae fuck Monkey, Davie's a regular."

"Where do you find these guys, Stevie?"

"Fuckin' Rock Steady Security. That agency's shite. Go on in Davie, I'll be in shortly. We need to talk."

"You're right we do, Stevie." Diller held his hands up and turned his face to let Stevie see the damage.

"Hondo?" Stevie asked.

Diller nodded, noticing a sharpness form in Stevie's eyes.

"Right, fuck this," Stevie growled

Throwing an arm around Diller, Stevie roared, "You're on yer own for the rest of the night, Monkey."

The pair bundled into a black taxi and headed for Stevie's flat.

# Chapter 12

## Private Dick

Scratching away in his notebook, Bowie made a show of sniffing deep breaths in through his nose. "You never think to clean this taxi out, Gallagher?"

The driver of the black Hackney cab was a balding forty year old, who'd been a pupil of Bowie's at Bellshill Academy in his youth and was subsequently immune to the man's gruffness.

"I do Mr Bowie," Gallagher said cheerfully, "but the smell of sick from the night-crawlers is hard to get out, y'know?"

Bowie wrinkled his nose further, looking around the interior of the cab as though he could see signs of disease dripping from its doors, ceiling and windows. He failed to notice Gallagher's eyes in the mirror wrinkle with a smile, watching him squirm.

"Just keep after that taxi, Gallagher," he instructed.

"Right you are, Mr Bowie." Gallagher shook his head and smiled to himself at his old teacher's eccentric behaviour.

Bowie, continuing to scribble in his notepad, craned his neck to keep watch on the private cab that he'd instructed Gallagher to follow from outside Angel's bar. Impatiently he dodged back and forth behind Gallagher's shiny head which kept bobbing around in the front of the cab, obscuring his view.

*A clown of a boy.* Bowie recalled Gallagher in his youth. *He's still a clown now. He should cover that head of his, it's bad manners walking the streets with a smooth head, shaved in like a bloody chimpanzee. A hat would be a start.*

Bowie tugged subconsciously at his toupee as he continued dodging Gallagher's head to keep the private cab in his line of sight. He didn't trust the clown not to lose it. Bowie was certain that tonight would be the night that he'd finally get some hard evidence on Davie Diller.

Deciding that Diller had been allowed to get away with far too much for far too long, Mr Bowie had begun following him around a few months ago. No one in Bellshill Academy, except himself of course, had spotted Diller for what he was. Lazy, irresponsible and downright dangerous. Diller angered and worried him in equal measures. Bowie had seen so many children go through *his* school that he'd developed a skill for seeing to the root of who a child really was; of who they would be. He saw it as his duty to make the best of the people in his care and remove those who were undesirable. Bowie had had no difficulty in spotting what Diller was, despite his smoothly executed display of cleverness and charm. Convinced Diller was a real danger to have in school, Bowie had committed to compiling a dossier of evidence to force the head teacher to kick him out, once and for all.

In the time Bowie had been following him around, Diller had spent most of his nights in and out of pubs and clubs. This irritated Mr Bowie, who was a firm believer in an early night, especially on a school night. He grew to resent Diller even more for forcing him to be out late at night too. On his nights out, Diller habitually met with a startling variety of types of people, drank late into the night and made a lot of female acquaintances. Whilst his night-time excursions were inappropriate, Bowie had to admit that he hadn't observed young Diller doing anything that he could use to get him kicked out of school. Until today, that is.

Mr Bowie had found himself with a free period that afternoon and decided to take a stroll around to the Cultural Centre to collect some new volumes of textbooks that the library had been kind enough to offer him. As he'd waited on the librarian, Bowie had taken a seat in the centre's little café with a coffee when he'd spotted Diller through the window. Smiling to himself, he retrieved his Diller logbook and noted the time he'd observed the supposedly sick Diller strolling casually past.

Deciding that a confrontation would warm his soul, Bowie left his coffee on the table and walked quickly out of the café, turning left towards the railway station, the direction he'd seen Diller take. He'd seen Diller's Adidas trainers, and he despised that footwear, disappear into the back of a van with two men. Bowie had only seen Diller's lower limbs go into the van, but he'd recognise the cocky walk and detestable trainers anywhere. *It doesn't look like he was too keen on going,* Bowie surmised from the shove he'd seen one of Diller's *friends* deliver.

Watching the rough-looking man turn around to scan the street and then enter the van, Bowie had a little chuckle to himself. Finally he'd caught a glimpse of Diller's involvement in what looked to be something illegal. Those men were known associates of that Hondo character. Heading back to school with a spring in his step, Bowie had decided to stake out Angel's on the chance that Diller would appear and that he could pile some more misery on him on what was obviously a bad day.

Sure enough Diller had turned up at the bar in the early evening looking bruised, pale, sick and sweaty, and wearing sticking plasters over the ends of swollen fingers. His appearance and lack of his usual composure brought a smile to Bowie's face. Watching him hail a cab with the doorman, Bowie had followed along, determined to find the dirt he needed. If he was being honest, Mr Bowie had to admit that it was fairly exciting, following someone you detested around, gathering evidence. It was like being a detective.

The private cab came to a halt outside a grubby flat on Glebe Street. Diller piled into the building with the doorman from Angel's, watched by Mr Bowie from the rear window of Gallagher's black cab.

"Drop me off round here, Gallagher," he instructed.

Driving off, Gallagher shook his head once again as he glanced in his mirror to see his former teacher take a hiding place in a bush.

After concealing himself and getting comfortable in the large shrubbery, Mr Bowie fished a small Laphroaig-filled hipper from the inside pocket of his tweed jacket and chugged down a generous measure. Swearing and muttering away to himself, he allowed the smallest and meanest of smiles to cross his lips at the thought of finally gaining the proof he needed to remove Diller, and in acknowledgement of his own ridiculous situation.

That he'd been reduced to following people around, hiding in bushes and scratching away in his notebook, was ridiculous, but Bowie reckoned that his actions were the only sane response to the environment he now found himself immersed in daily.

Having begun teaching in the early seventies, Bowie had entered the profession at a time when all of the power was in the hands of the teachers, as was correct in his view. Children had known their place in those days, at home as well as in school, where any misdemeanour was dealt with quickly and effectively. Corporally.

Since corporal punishment had been phased out in the UK in the early eighties, Bowie had watched the power swing decisively and irreversibly from teacher to pupil. Children who'd once been too frightened to display anything other than obedience, manners and acquiescence, now brazenly walked the school corridors with no fear of anyone or anything. They dropped litter at their arses. They smoked right at the front of the school gates and scowled at anyone who looked in their direction. They pushed past teachers in corridors and dared anyone to challenge them.

Where lessons had once been academic in nature and focused on gaining knowledge and skills, they were now focused on the *experience of the learner*. Current teaching practice asserted that so long as the experience was good, the outcome, the knowledge gained, was of secondary importance.

Pupils in his classes had once been rigidly disciplined and had learned their lessons the hard way, but learn them they had. Now he had kids sitting in his class who couldn't spell their own name, but could build the hell out of a papier-mâché tower.

Bowie had given up hoping that the good old days when he was allowed to be effective would ever come back, and had to admit that whilst he'd like corporal punishment to be reintroduced, it would never happen. Hell, if he laid a finger on one of these kids today, they'd kick the shite out of him in return.

The internet, iPhones, BBM, e-mail, Blu-Ray, portable hard-drives, Smart-boards, iPads, Power-Point, data projectors, learning support assistants, behaviour support assistants, interventions, child psychologists, learning intentions, kinaesthetic/audio/visual learners, ADHD, dyslexia, dyspraxia, ODD, dysgraphia – these were the tools and the business of the modern teacher. More and more it did seem to Bowie that school had become a business and not a service.

Young teachers these days spoke like a cross between a social worker, a lawyer, a psychiatrist and a business man (excuse me, business person), but not a teacher. At seventy-two years old, former soldier Bowie was a fossil in this world, but despite being eligible for over a decade, couldn't face retiring. Not yet.

He needed to be in charge, to be useful, but felt less so with every day that passed in the madhouse that had once been such a place of comfort and support for him. People whom he'd once mentored, whom he'd introduced to teaching and supported when classes or workload or discipline had become too much, had now surpassed him on the career ladder and looked at him in meetings like they would a senile elder; all patronising smiles and allowances.

*Diller.*

If he could show them what Diller really was, he'd be able to regain some of the respect he'd lost, be able to contribute confidently and have his opinion valued once more.

Bowie took another long chug of the Laphroaig and warmed his chest whilst he looked up at the second-floor flat with his target inside, absent-mindedly scratching underneath his toupee as he muttered, "I see you, ye wee bastard. I'll make everyone see you."

# Chapter 13

## Fatboy Slim

Leaving Glebe Street in a private cab, Diller sank with a sigh into the soft leather rear seat of the Ford Mondeo. The driver's eyes flicked to the mirror.

"You all right, Davie?"

Diller narrowed his eyes to focus on the driver. Realising that he knew the man, another Bellshill Academy alumni, Diller relaxed once more.

"Oh, aye, I'm fine Johnny. How you doing yerself?"

"Just working away," Johnny replied. "Where we going?"

"Bothwell Bridge, Johnny," Diller replied.

"Will the hotel car park do you?"

Diller nodded and broke eye contact, a sign that the conversation was over. He knew Johnny quite well, but wasn't in the mood for small talk. He had a lot to think about. Johnny took the hint and switched on Gina McKie's late night programme on Radio Clyde. Whilst Johnny listened to some guy tell Gina about his marriage problems and drove, Diller schemed silently in the back of the cab.

Arriving at the Bothwell Bridge Hotel, Johnny switched the meter off.

"Eight pound fifty, Davie," he chirped, still giggling from the guy's conversation with Gina.

Twisting around, he noted that Diller's attention was miles away and spoke a little louder.

"Davie." Diller's head snapped up. "That's us, Davie."

"Aw, right. Thanks, Johnny." Diller handed him a ten pound note. "Catch ye around, eh?" Diller slammed the door behind him and watched Johnny poke a wave through his open window as he drove off.

Straightening his clothes a little, Diller turned and headed towards Hoylake Park, a residential street which lay around a mile and a half from the hotel. Taking his time, Diller arrived forty minutes later at a very large, very modern house with a blue Maserati Quattroporte parked in its driveway, sat alongside a white Range Rover Evoque. Instead of knocking the door, Diller retrieved his iPhone, found the number he wanted in his contacts and texted a message to say that he was outside the recipient's house. Five minutes later, Chubbs Valenti appeared, looking half-asleep in his white Caesar's Palace robe.

"Sorry, Fran. Did I wake you?" Diller asked.

"Not at all, Dah-vid." Despite being born and bred in Lanarkshire, Francesco Valenti frequently injected a little bit of Italy into his accent. Half the time he sounded like an Italian trying to do a Scot's accent, or vice versa.

"I was jeest-ah watching the telly. Come in."

Guiding Diller through to a massive and well-equipped kitchen, Chubbs set about making each of them an espresso, before asking, "You have news for me, Dah-vid?"

Diller stroked his stubbled face, choosing his words.

"I'm in the shit, Fran."

Chubbs perched himself on a tall stool. Sucking down his espresso in one smooth movement, he offered Diller a wee salute with his cup, indicating *it's good, no?* In response Diller drained the bitter coffee from his own cup and gave Chubbs a thumbs-up.

"I'm hungry," Chubbs announced. Stepping from his stool he strode to the American-style fridge that stood monstrously against the wall closest to Diller. Throwing packs of continental meats, cheeses, tomatoes, salads and dressings onto the closest counter, Chubbs retrieved some ciabatta from a cupboard and a large chopping knife, and set about constructing a meal for both of them.

"Are you hungry, Dah-vid?" he asked over his shoulder as he sliced open the bread.

Despite his frame of mind, Diller laughed to himself. Fran had been given the nickname Chubbs as a kid, not because he was overweight, but due to his massive height and stick-thin body, despite eating non-stop his entire life. Diller couldn't recall ever having spent time in Chubb's company when the man hadn't had food in his mouth. He liked Chubbs, liked him a lot, actually. The man's vitality was infectious.

The son of a steelworker, *wasn't everyone in Lanarkshire*, who had been affectionately nicknamed Tally Valenti, Chubbs was third-generation Scots-Italian; Peroni in one hand, Glenmorangie in the other.

He'd made his money by importing olive oil into the UK from Tuscany in the nineties when continental eating had started to become popular, even in Lanarkshire. Eventually branching out into coffee in the noughties, Chubbs had made global contacts along with a shit-load of money. He used those contacts and logistics infrastructures to begin importing and shipping cocaine overland and overseas into Europe and the UK from South America.

Why he'd stayed in Lanarkshire, in his expensive but unassuming house in Bothwell, Diller couldn't guess. Chubbs certainly had enough money to live how and where he chose. Maybe it was the danger. Diller could relate.

Whilst Chubbs was a man with influence and reach, he exuded little in the way of real power or threat. Chubbs had always relied on his genial personality and infallible network to shield him from the people he supplied. He thought of himself as indisposable, irreplaceable in his role as supplier. There was always an element of nervousness in Chubbs' manner. For a man in his position, he was really more of a manager, a bean counter or a facilitator than a genuinely feared member of the underworld. Chubbs was fearful of the people he supplied, but the appeal of either the money or the danger his role presented appeared to have overridden the anxiety he so obviously felt.

Chubbs was the main supplier to almost every top level coke dealer in Scotland and most of Northern England, including Hondo. As such he was vital to Diller's plans, although he didn't know it. Chubbs thought of Diller as a friend; someone who wanted to learn from the great man in business, yes, but also a genuine friend. Whilst Diller had learned much from his would-be mentor, he was there simply for appearances. He'd built a relationship with Chubbs for the same reason that he'd taken so much of Hondo's coke and thrown it around with such abandon. He'd done these things with the single intention of provoking Hondo.

"Aye, thanks, Fran. That'd be great." As he said it, Diller realised that the last food he'd eaten had been breakfast with his mother, which at this moment felt like a month ago. His stomach growled at him in protest and anticipation.

"*Molto buono*!" Chubbs announced with gusto, patting his flat abdomen. "I think better with food in my stomach."

"Look, Fran…" Diller managed to look genuinely worried.

Chubbs held an index finger straight up, to silence Diller. "Food first, *amico*, and then we talk. Ok?"

Mopping up some oil with the last of his ciabatta, Chubbs' mind at last turned to business.

"What's-ah the story then, Dah-vid?"

Diller stuffed some antipasti in his mouth, making Chubbs wait for a minute or so whilst he chewed and picked his words. "Hondo took me to the steelworks today." Diller held his hands up to show Chubbs his fingertips.

"Fuck sake, Davie. Why would he do this to you?" Chubbs sat forward in concern, taking a closer look at Diller's fingertips, all trace of Italy gone from his Lanarkshire accent.

"It's hard to say, Fran," Diller replied. "He's decided that I owe him a hundred grand."

Chubbs whistled through his teeth in reply. "How long has he given you to get his money to him?"

Diller raised an eyebrow and smiled ironically. "Friday. He wants it by Friday."

Fran lit two cigarettes and handed one to Diller. Both smoked quietly for a while until Chubbs broke the silence.

"He thinks that I'm setting you up with my contacts. We've been stupid; I should've just told Hondo that we've become friends."

Diller shook his head, fought back a smile and forced his eyes to moisten. "Nah, it's only about his money, Fran. He wants the money."

Fran's voice was growing more concerned and more Scottish by the second. "Hondo's been in this business for a long time. He basically invented it; he's seen it all before, Davie. He thinks he's being fucked by us. He's going to kill you, or me, or both of us." Chubbs was on his feet, lighting a second cigarette. "We're fucked, Davie. We're fucked. These people don't tolerate competition."

Diller watched Chubbs as he lost his composure and made himself ignore the rising disgust he felt towards the *Italian*.

"I'm going to phone him and try to sort this mess out," Chubbs squealed, heading for the phone.

This Diller hadn't expected and couldn't allow. He needed Hondo to remain at arm's length, mistrustful of Chubbs. He needed Hondo to be angry and worried about who was planning what. He needed Hondo reacting instead of thinking. With one call, Chubbs would blow any chance his plan had of succeeding.

Over several months Diller had successfully driven a wedge of suspicion, fear and mistrust between the old colleagues, but he'd expected Chubbs to react to his news in a much meeker manner, perhaps disappearing to the continent for a few weeks; that was his usual style. He'd obviously pushed Chubbs too hard, or perhaps Chubbs' relationship with Hondo had more depth than he'd suspected. Either way, Chubbs hadn't reacted as he'd hoped. His response to the situation had been much more proactive than Diller had foreseen. Diller quickly reassessed his next move.

As he watched Chubbs reach for his phone, Diller felt a coldness creep across him, then he instantly relaxed. He began mentally sorting through all of the possibilities and options that lay ahead. Instantly analysing cause and effect of this action or that, of the likely benefits or disadvantages that changes to his plans may reap, Diller made his choice five seconds later. Two seconds after that, Chubbs' favourite kitchen knife was buried in his chest, severing his aorta.

Diller held him gently, like a dance partner, and reclined his skinny body onto the expensive tiles, watching Chubbs' eyes the whole time and soaking up the fear, anger, disbelief and finally blankness of his expression. He hadn't come here to harm his *friend*, he'd intended only to move some pieces of the chess board further apart, but circumstances had determined that business required Chubbs be removed.

"Sorry, Chubbs, but you'd only have fucked everything up."

Diller spent the next hour meticulously scrubbing, bleaching, and wiping surfaces, removing all traces of his presence from Chubbs' home, phone and his body. Normally he'd have disposed of the body in the same manner that he did with all of his other kills: burning and a shallow grave in the middle of a nearby forest. In Chubbs' case, he wanted the man found. He wanted fallout. He wanted to send a message to Hondo: *Chubbs isn't a problem anymore, and so neither is Diller.* It might cause Hondo to doubt the actions he'd chosen, or it might set him more firmly on his chosen path. It was worth a stab.

Slipping out the back door into the garden, Diller took a last look at Chubbs. "Thanks for dinner, Fran."

\*\*\*\*\*\*\*\*\*\*\*\*\*\*\*\*\*\*

Three minutes after Diller left the tidy garden, Mr Bowie, looking angry, uncomfortable and confused, stepped out from between two Scots Pine trees. Cracking the stiffness from his knees, Bowie took a long chug on his hip flask, enjoying the burn in his throat and chest, and then checked his watch. Two am. Shaking his head, Bowie straightened his wig and staggered from the garden to approach the kitchen window of Chubbs' house.

Bowie had gotten angrier and more drunken as the night had progressed. Following Diller around all night, hiding in bushes, trees and behind walls, and growing more tired and hungry as the hours crawled past had robbed him of all his fantasies and pretentions of being a PI. Swearing loudly, Bowie dragged a barrel-styled garden seat over to the house's kitchen window, wincing as his chest muscles complained at the effort. Finally he climbed on top and nervously peeked inside.

The old teacher scanned around the still brightly-lit kitchen, admiring how orderly and clean it had been kept. Lovely spice racks, jars and bottles arranged neatly, labels uniformly facing front. He imagined cupboards filled with condiments and tins, all standing to the same, neat attention and smiled with approval.

Flicking his eyes to the counter nearest the fridge, Bowie noticed a selection of meats, cheeses, bread, oils, vinegars and fruit presented in a serving dish. His stomach growled at him and heartburn seared his chest. He hadn't eaten since leaving school this afternoon. Spirits finally flagging and hunger winning out, Bowie decided to go home. He was feeling every day of his seventy-two years at that moment.

As he began to step off from his makeshift stool, Mr Bowie noticed someone's foot and ankle sticking out from the furthermost wall. The wall concealed the rest of what he presumed was a person. Bowie headed straight for the back door.

Trying the handle, Mr Bowie was pleased to feel it give under the pressure from his hand. Suddenly very sober and alert, he slowly crept into Chubbs' house.

"Hello? Is everybody all right in here?" Imagining someone ill or perhaps an elderly person who'd taken a fall, he forced his voice to sound calm and reassuring: his teacher's voice.

"My name is Mr Bowie, I'm just checking to see if you're all right."

As Bowie cleared the corner wall, he found Chubbs and gasped. The man was on his back with a twelve-inch kitchen knife plunged into his chest. There was a lake of blood around him, but the absorbent house coat he wore had prevented it from spreading more than two inches from him. The robe, once white, was now almost completely red, making the Caesar's Palace emblem blaze out from its cloth.

Feeling his breath tighten, Bowie went into automatic pilot. It was obvious that the man was dead, but he started CPR anyway. As he moved from breathing to compressions, Bowie tugged on the knife handle to remove it, sending a splatter of blood over his face and chest from the freshly removed blade. Tossing the knife aside, Mr Bowie began pumping on Chubbs' chest and blowing air into his mouth.

Over and over he pushed and blew, blood squeezing through the wound and out of the man's mouth with each push. Breathing again, Mr Bowie turned to watch the man's chest rise as he blew a lungful of air uselessly in again. Eventually he noticed the frothy blood bubbles appear on the side of the man's chest each time he filled his lungs. Watching his own breath leak from this man's chest and form a horrific blood bubble which popped as cheerfully as any soapy one, Bowie gave up and sat back on his feet, suddenly overcome with long-forgotten memories of battlefield wounds and trauma he'd thought had left him.

Images of horrors from decades before, burned into his brain in Northern Ireland and The Falklands, each as vivid as any 3D Marvel movie, flashed before his eyes. Limbs, organs and tissue spattered by and on him, like it was happening again, right here, right now. Bowie tried to force the memories back to wherever they'd been hidden for so long but found that, like escaped prisoners, they were out of their restraints and they weren't going back again. Not for anything or anyone. He shifted his focus to the man in front of him.

*Diller. David Diller did this.*

The realisation brought one last surge of panic and finally filled him with relief in the form of a massive heart attack and a stroke. Combined, they took Bowie far from any conscious thought.

Mark Wilson

# THURSDAY

Mark Wilson

# Chapter 14

## Gerry's Fuckin' Place

Finding that he was too wired from his visit to Chubbs, Diller had been grateful for the text from Gerry 'fuckin' Malone that had popped through as he strolled back to the Bothwell Bridge Hotel.

'Gerry's got a shitload of coke and a couple of lonely ladies at his house. Coming?'

For once, Gerry had perfect 'fuckin' timing. Diller called a cab to take him the short journey to Gerry's flat in Hamilton Park, next to Hamilton Racecourse.

Diller checked his phone: 5:45 am. Groaning, he welcomed Thursday morning's arrival by throwing up in the drawer under the very luxurious 'And So To Bed' King-sized bed in Gerry's spare room. Rising to stand on weak legs, Diller heeled the drawer shut before heading through to Gerry's living room.

The previous night had been an unexpectedly brilliant experience. Diller couldn't remember the last time he'd laughed so hard. Gerry 'fuckin' Malone was, when separated from his chinless comrades, great 'fuckin' company. The girls Gerry had lined up had sat bored, whilst he and Diller discussed music, real music for a change, past conquests and the drug scene. Scowling, the girls eventually left, unnoticed, an hour later.

Gerry, as it turned out, wasn't the fool that he pretended to be. Having entered into the corporate world, qualification-free, Gerry had worked his arse off, worked hard and learned to walk and talk like his colleagues but had managed to continue thinking like a human being. The guy was very clever and understood people and their motivations much more deeply than Diller would have previously thought possible. Driven to succeed in an environment that he hated, Gerry, with his mask of respectability and communality and his limitless ambition, had forced and manoeuvred himself into a position in his sector that many of his more educated colleagues would kill to attain. In contrast with the persona he displayed around his peers, Gerry was wickedly funny, had genuine warmth for people he liked, but was absolutely nobody's fool. He was also a ruthless bastard when it came to getting what he wanted.

For the first time since Paul had died, Diller felt that there was someone in the world who he could relate to. Of course, Gerry didn't have a clue what Diller was really like, but that needn't always be the case. Part of Diller was tired of constantly lying, of hiding who he really was beneath a mask of conformity and he longed to simply be himself with someone. Was that even possible when you were a bastard of Diller's calibre? Diller thought not, but was considering showing Gerry who he really was, and seeing how he reacted. Maybe Stacey had been right, maybe he did need to let someone be a friend to him.

Finding that Gerry was fast asleep on the couch, Diller made himself a bowl of porridge, ate quickly and left to catch the early bus home to change for school.

The night buses in Lanarkshire were always an adventure. Filled with drunkards, pissed-off guys who hadn't scored at the clubs the night before and the occasional mystified tourist, they weren't for the faint-hearted but provided entertainment like no other. On previous journeys Diller had encountered lunatics of all varieties, bricks through windows (when passing through Viewpark), couples arguing, crying or shagging, junkies smacked out of their heads on the floor of the bus, rolling to and fro, blissfully unaware as the bus chugged through the streets, and teenagers smashing their bodies over seats and against windows and floors in 'Jackass' style. Diller often wondered why First Bus bothered to run the service; surely the cost of damage outweighed any profit from the busy bus, but run it they did. For Diller, the night bus was a necessity.

The first First Bus bus of the day that Diller had caught was quiet compared to what could have been expected on the bus that had run through the estates just an hour previously, the final night bus. Aside from Diller the bus held only two other passengers. One was a tramp snoozing happily, nursing a brown-bag-covered bottle of gut-rot. He looked like he'd spent the night travelling around Lanarkshire in the back of the bus and was curled up on the back seat, his bottle for a teddy bear.

The bus's other occupant sat to the left of Diller, three rows forward. In her late forties, with short, blonde hair and beautiful, large brown eyes surrounded by gorgeous laughter lines, Diller found himself sitting watching her for a good ten minutes. Dressed in fashionable denims and blazer, she sat with her back pushed up against her seat and her body folded so that her feet rested on her seat, heels against her bum and her knees pushed against the seat in front.

Blondie, the very definition of multi-tasking, was juggling between swigging from a bottle of Peroni, rolling herself a cigarette from a pouch filled with cigarette papers, filters and Gold Leaf tobacco, and clicking away on the keypad of a white Blackberry with her thumbs. Every time her Blackberry buzzed, she'd balance her beer between her knees, snatch up her phone and laugh softly as she read the message.

Her laughter lines engaged and her eyes lit up as she smiled. She was beautiful: beautiful and hopeful. Her story was conveyed by her every action, her appearance and her demeanour.

In a reflective mood, Diller watched manicured nails on nimble fingers alternate between rolling thin, tidy little cigarettes and tapping out her next reply on a well-worn keyboard. He took in her every action and reaction and watched her story unfold. Peroxide blonde hair and beautiful laughter lines enhanced a face that had so obviously seen so much disappointment, but whose eyes sparkled with the hope of a new love.

A middle-aged divorcee, she'd obviously been out all night and was exchanging 'next day' emails or texts with her date. Eventually she packed her things away, smiling, and dabbed on some make-up before stepping out into the Bellshill morning, filled with hope that *this* time was *the* time. That *he* was what she'd been waiting for. Diller tended to sneer at people like Blondie, but the obvious warmth and dignity that she radiated simply made him smile. It reminded him of Gerry in strange way.

School that day passed in a blur, mostly because Mr Bowie hadn't turned up for work. Diller had completed a series of classes that he'd actually quite enjoyed as well as a talk he'd promised Mr

McLatchie, the head teacher, for the first years on the importance of Remembrance Day. Without the pressure of having Bowie peering over his shoulder all day, school actually became a positive place to be. The afterglow from the fun he'd had hours before had also helped to keep his fatigue at bay. By the end of the school day, Diller had gotten his second wind and had left school feeling hopeful and invigorated.

Stevie had done his best to put Diller's mind at rest last night. It had been quite endearing listening to Stevie's *we'll do this, try that, sort this* rhetoric. All of Stevie's plans were focused on protecting Diller, on making Hondo back off, on getting Diller out of the life he was *trapped* in. It had been riotously funny from Diller's point of view, but that was as useful as Stevie was now to Diller, entertainment.

Aside from his role at Angel's, Stevie's usefulness had diminished in recent months. Where once he'd conveyed a steady stream of information from Hondo and from his ex-colleagues, Stevie had now pissed off too many of his *brother officers* with his on-going bitterness towards all things *polis,* and subsequently had only Dougie remaining as a friend. Allowing Stevie to snitch to Hondo had made it possible for Diller to throw some bogus information Hondo's way and been useful in keeping Hondo's attention focused elsewhere, like worrying about why he was meeting with Chubbs or how he was going through such large amounts of Coke. It would appear Stevie's conscience had finally gotten the better of him now, so his usefulness in that regard had come to an end. As far as Hondo was concerned, though, former DS Steven Miller would have one final useful function to perform.

Diller spent the rest of the day doing the rounds, visiting his street dealers in their various locations and collecting his cut from them. Saving Kenzo's former patch until last, he eventually met with Weasel who had taken Kenzo's role effortlessly. Takings were up already under Weasel's charge. Congratulating his team, Diller Caught a 44 bus and travelled to the Parkhead Forge. By the time Diller got there, he'd decided to go to the cinema to escape reality for a couple of hours.

Friday's confrontation was getting closer and he needed to give his mind a rest from the constant scheming and calculating he'd been doing for the last few weeks. Opting for *Iron Man 3*, Diller lost himself for two hours in the fun and action the movie offered. By the time Diller left the cinema at 23:00, he had only one destination in mind.

Arriving at Holytown Crematorium almost ninety minutes later, Diller walked slowly along Memorial Place and scaled the short, black gates which closed off the memorial garden. Just walking through the garden towards the spot where Paul's plaque stood filled Diller with anger and sadness. Each step he took brought a stab of memory from the past. Paul's too-small, white coffin; Uncle Cameron and David's own dad, dressed in black, holding Cameron up; Cameron holding his wife, Auntie Rose holding the smaller kids. When the coffin had slid creepily along its rollers and into the awaiting furnace, Auntie Rose had fallen to the chapel floor and wailed endlessly. It had seemed endless at any rate.

David had gone into himself by then, shutting himself off from everything that was taking place around him. He concentrated on the little knife he'd taken from his grandfather's tobacco pouch. Blunt as it was from years of scraping the old man's pipe, it still felt good, and clean, and right as he tore and slid it discreetly down and into the skin on his palm. Feeling the cold metal and then the warm release of the blood had given something for David to focus on, an escape from the horrors around him, a release valve.

Walking along the stony path towards Paul's plaque, Diller bent his middle finger under his thumb to form an 'O' and squeezed his nail-less fingertip, using the pain to push the memories away and back into the steel trap-box where he'd forced so many memories and emotions in the past. Lighting a Marl-borough Light, Diller squatted down to sweep some moss from the plaque with his hand, then he sat down to smoke and to talk.

Explaining the position that he was in to Paul, he told his dead cousin all of his plans. Discussing the variables he was trying to predict, influence and control, Diller had laughed out loud many times during the one-sided conversation, acknowledging how precariously balanced his future was. Several events and encounters had to play out just right over the coming twenty-four hours, otherwise he'd be out of business or he'd be dead. If Diller was as clever as everyone seemed to think he was, he might survive this thing; better, he might thrive.

Standing, Diller brushed his denims clean of dirt and moss from the ground, kissed his fingers and planted the moisture from his lips onto Paul's plaque.

"Maybe see you soon, Cuz."

Feeling calm and in control of the coming events, Diller straightened his back and went home. Sleep was calling.

Mark Wilson

# Chapter 15

## The 104 Pick-Up

"You should let me kill this guy, Dad."

Dragging his mill file from blade to handle along the relief edge of his Bowie knife, Hondo looked over the top of his glasses to regard his son. After giving the boy a hard stare, Hondo turned back to his task before replying, "I said no, Lionel."

"Dad, you should have seen him in that chair after you left; smiling at me, laughing at me as I pulled his nails out. I've never seen anything like it. He's dangerous, Dad. He's a creepy bastard."

Hondo sighed and loosened the vice that had been holding his blade by its handle. Making Lionel wait, he checked the uniformity along the edge of the blade meticulously, turned it over and placed it carefully back into the vice, facing the other direction. Once more he retrieved his file and began slowly working in a smooth sweep from edge to handle at a shallow angle. Most folk wouldn't go near their knife with a mill file for fear of damaging the edge of the blade. Most would prefer a whet stone, but a large survival knife like a Bowie needed special care.

As much for use as an axe or a hammer as it was as a knife, the big, heavy Bowie knife had traditionally been used for chopping, skinning, cleaving bone or for stabbing. The Bowie had been an outdoorsman's knife, a fighter's knife. Hondo had used his Bowie for each of these purposes, and many others besides. A blade as busy as his had been over the years needed caring for.

Lionel shifted his feet and clattered around impatiently, arranging stacks of cash, preparing them for transportation to Green Billy's. Whilst Lionel stomped and banged around like a moody teenager, Hondo released the Bowie from the vice once more, inspected it and then sat to begin the final phase of sharpening with his whet stone.

Spitting on the coarse side of his stone, Hondo moved once more from tip to palm using small circular movements along the edge. He found this a more effective method of sharpening the relief edge of a Bowie than using a traditional drag along the stone. As his blade sang against the stone he cocked an eyebrow and spoke calmly.

"We'll see what tomorrow brings, Lionel."

Lionel wasn't impressed. "Why, Dad? We know what he's planning, he wants our business. I know he's a good salesman but there are plenty others who can learn to sell like him. I could give ye half a dozen names off the top of my head right now, and none of them are as dangerous as this freak."

Hondo returned to his blade. Raising it to eye level he placed the hammer-like handle near to his nose, pointed the tip away from him and looked along the edge once more. Turning his stone over Hondo spat forcefully on the fine side and began repeating his circular movements along the blade, each stroke calming him.

"Lionel, you know why."

Hurt flashing momentarily in his eyes, Lionel looked away from his dad.

"Aye. Look, Dad, I know I'm not the brightest but I've been in this business wi' you almost my whole life. I know what I'm doing, and I can always take someone on to do the number crunching." Lionel looked at his dad with a mixture of anger and pleading.

"No," Hondo stated simply. "When I'm gone, you'll need a partner; someone with knowledge of how the business works as well as the smarts to take it forward. I want Diller, but only if he can be made to do as he's told."

"You haven't been listening to me." Lionel thumped the nearest cash pile with his fist in anger.

Despite the seriousness of their conversation, Hondo had to smile in recognition of how many times in the past he, as a father, had said that exact phrase to his son. Following a mistake, accident or act of deliberate disobedience by Lionel, Hondo had been on the boy in a flash, chastising him. *You haven't been listening to me, son.*

In hindsight he'd been hard on the boy, too hard. Despite many meetings with and letters from Lionel's teachers at Bellshill Academy about the boy's *difficulties*, despite phrases like ADHD and dyslexia thrown at Lionel, Hondo had been convinced that the boy had just been lazy, that he needed a good kick up the arse, like he'd had himself as a kid from his old man.

Hondo had been blind to Lionel's problems and had made his son's teenage years a miserable litany of failure and disappointment lived to the soundtrack of his father's disapproving voice, *try harder, do better, be better, can't you just do it right?* Young Lionel's physicality had been his saving grace. The only place the boy could do anything right in those days had been on the rugby pitch. Lionel had been a brilliant hooker. His strength and single-minded determination on the field made him a popular and talented player.

When Lionel turned sixteen and school ended, a few scouts from regional clubs had called on him, but by that time Lionel had decided that the best way he could earn his father's respect was to work with him. Hondo, to his shame, hadn't tried too hard to talk him into sticking in at the rugby, primarily because he needed someone with his son's physical presence that he could trust. His sister Helen had been right, though. Hondo should never have brought his son into his world.

In those days, Hondo had still felt bitter about the path his career and life had taken. He'd had a chip on his shoulder and hate in his heart. Having watched his relatives work their days there, he'd never expected to leave the steelworks. He'd expected a job for life. When redundancy came, Hondo had felt disillusioned and betrayed. He simply wanted to scream *fuck you* to the system and had put every ounce of his considerable will into creating for himself a position that no one would ever take from him. The years had taught him the price of his choices, and the guilt for what he'd turned his son into weighed heaviest of all on him.

Still, despite his regrets, he was who and what he was, and he'd worked hard for what he had. Lionel needed someone to help him or he needed to get out of the business when Hondo was done with this life. There was no way that his son would leave the business behind. Lionel saw it as his only link to his father, as the only way he could prove his worth to a father he felt didn't value him.

Hondo's smile vanished into sadness. Lionel grabbed his stone-hand to prevent him scraping around in circles.

"Diller will not be told. He won't do what you want him to do, Dad. We don't need a guy like this in our lives."

Releasing the stone, Hondo rotated his wrist and closed his hand around Lionel's. "Unfortunately we do need him, Lionel." *Because you're a fuck-up.* Hondo didn't say it, but they both heard it in their heads regardless.

Pulling his hand free, Lionel left the cash-filled basement and stormed off upstairs to re-join a paused game of *Call of Duty* on his X-Box.

Hondo stood, shouting after him, "If he doesn't get in line, he's all yours, son."

Retrieving a Smith's pull-through sharpener from a shelf, he pulled the Bowie's relief edge through the ceramic side of the sharpener. This final process made the blade razor sharp. The sharpness wouldn't last for long on a Bowie, but the groundwork he'd put in with the mill file and the whet stone meant that a very sharp blade lay below the razor-sharpness. With a hefty knife like this one, very sharp was good enough.

Hondo fetched two packs of playing cards from a drawer. Stacking them neatly on a metal table mat on top of his scarred workbench, he swung a casual chop down on top of the one hundred and four cards, slicing lazily and easily through both decks. The Bowie knife slid through the metal plate and came to a halt a quarter of an inch into the bench. Hondo called this test, which he performed each time he sharpened his blade, 'The 104 Pick-up'.

Tomorrow was Friday. He was ready. Diller damn well better be ready too. One way or another, this nonsense would be over in twenty-four hours.

"Dad, come up here. You've got to see this," Lionel yelled down the basement stairs to Hondo. It had been an hour since Lionel had stormed off and Hondo had spent the time reading to give the boy some space.

Packing away his current read, *The Fix* by Keith Nixon, Hondo smiled and began strolling up towards the living room.

"I've paused it for you, Dad," Lionel told him as he entered the room.

Taking his 'readers' off, Hondo narrowed his eyes and peered at the TV. Lionel had paused the STV Scottish news bulletin. *Christ, was it ten thirty-five already?*

"Right son, stick it on." Hondo nodded at the telly.

Lionel hit the play button and watched as his father's face fell in disbelief during the two-minute bulletin.

A reporter stood, shielded by a large, cheerily-coloured golf brolly, outside a familiar looking modern house, relaying information from the police.

"This afternoon, in this quiet little estate where kids play around in the road, a body was discovered in the home of Francesco Valenti, a fifty-one-year-old businessman."

Hondo sat the edge of his backside on a chair and hunched forward, hands clasped, elbows resting on his knees.

"Discovered early this afternoon by Mary Murphy, his cleaner, the body has been identified as the house's owner, Mr Valenti, who appears to have been stabbed through the heart with a kitchen knife."

Hondo's mouth curved down at the sides and his eyebrows rose in reaction.

"Also discovered unconscious at the scene was seventy-two-year-old Bellshill Academy Principle Teacher of English, Mr Duncan Bowie. Mr Bowie, a former Royal Marine and teacher of some forty years, was, according to Mrs Murphy, unconscious, and covered in blood. The head teacher at the school declined to comment, saying only that Mr Bowie hadn't turned up for work today."

The reporter was replaced onscreen by DCI Douglas Diller who, as the senior officer on scene, and was preparing to give a statement.

"Preliminary forensics reports suggest…" DCI Diller checked his notes again and coughed uncomfortably, "reports suggest that Mr Bowie stabbed Mr Valenti in the heart. We are treating the case as murder and will question Mr Bowie if and when he recovers from what appears to have been a significant heart attack as well as a stroke."

Hondo sat open-mouthed as DCI Douglas responded to a few questions.

"No we don't have any other suspects… Yes, Mr Bowie's fingerprints have been found on the murder weapon… No, we don't have a motive, the men wouldn't appear to have had any links before now…"

DCI Diller soon tired of the reporters and left them standing shouting their questions at an empty mike stand as the camera switched back to the reporter.

"This is Julia Bain, reporting from Hoylake Park, Bothwell, where a murder case involving a respected local teacher has stunned the community. Back to the studio."

Hondo turned to Lionel. "That the same Bowie who taught you? The one at Diller's school?"

"Aye," Lionel replied. "He's a prick."

Hondo nodded. "He's a prick who just did us a massive favour."

\*\*\*\*\*\*\*\*\*\*\*\*\*\*\*\*\*\*

Douglas turned from the pack of reporters and stomped back into Fran Valenti's home, sighing heavily in frustration. With Duncan Bowie's involvement, this case was just too close to home for Dougie's liking. The man had been young David's English teacher in fifth year; hell, David saw him at school every day. He'd told Dougie many times that Mr Bowie was unreasonably hard on him, *a fucking nutcase*. A lifelong educator, even in the Royal Marines, Duncan Bowie had been an instructor. He was a hard man, no doubt about it, but he'd always seemed a good man to Douglas. As difficult as it was to believe it of a man like Mr Bowie, the evidence in front of him showed Douglas that there had been much more to Duncan Bowie than anyone knew. Aside from the blood, the fingerprints and his unexplained presence in Valenti's house, the notebooks they'd found in the English teacher's pocket had been enough to convince Douglas that Mr Bowie wasn't who he'd thought he was.

DC Whitelaw's daft dog, Muffin, had detected a substantial quantity of cocaine in a hidden compartment under the master bedroom's floorboards. Valenti had never been on the CID's radar. They'd never had any reason to connect him with anything illegal. A haul of cocaine the size of the one that Dougie's men had discovered on the property, showed him that Valenti had been a major supplier, maybe even *the* major supplier in the area.

Whitelaw had also discovered the notebooks, handing them straight to Douglas without reading them. Luckily. Dougie's heart had begun thumping the moment he read the inside title page of the notebook numbered 'One'.

## David Diller Surveillance Log

Douglas had snapped the notebook shut and had barked at Whitelaw. "Clear the room and take yer fuckin' dug with ye."

Whitelaw and his colleagues gathered around the crime scene were stunned at their normally laid-back DCI's outburst. Despite his puzzled expression, Whitelaw quickly did as he was commanded.

As soon as he had the room to himself, Douglas began inspecting the notebooks. Three in total, the A5, hardback books were held shut by elastic bands wrapped around each one individually. Douglas opened the book designated *Book One* once again and began scanning through its pages.

Laid out with time, date and comments as headings, each page was part of a meticulous log maintained for over three months. Douglas wiped some sweat from his top lip with the back of his gloved hand and skipped through, scanning every other page.

***Arrived at such and such: 22:30, departed from here or there: 09:00.***

Page after page of details of where Douglas' son had been spending his days and nights. The comments were little more than questions or exclamations of intent from Bowie in most cases, occasionally becoming rants about how he'd show everyone what Diller was up to.

***What's he doing here at this hour?***
***On a school night?***
***The arrogant little bastard!***

Douglas read and re-read each notebook over an hour or so and found nothing that explained why Bowie had chosen to stalk his son. No theories, no accusations, just dates, times and rants. Douglas wasn't keen on the hours his son kept or the places he visited, but he was old enough to decide for himself. *What the hell was this maniac doing following him around?*

As he decided to close the books over, Douglas noticed two pages stuck together near the final entry in notebook 'Three'. Prising them apart, Douglas noted a comment in Bowie's fastidiously neat handwriting that took his fear and anger to a whole new level.

### *Abducted by James Crosbie's men*

As uncomfortable as Douglas had been about the case previously, finding the notebooks had made his brain bypass *interested copper* and go straight to *protective and angry father*.

Noting that David's name appeared in only one place, the beginning of Book One, he ripped the first page out and stuck it into his trouser pocket before furiously crashing through the door to re-join his subordinates. Tossing the three notebooks into the evidence box, Douglas whipped around to face the busy team who were gathering evidence.

"When that bastard wakes up, I want to be contacted immediately. Got it?" Douglas roared.

Five heads snapped up from five tasks and nodded in unison.

"*Before* anyone else. I want to be the first person to interview Duncan Bowie," he shouted over his shoulder as he stormed towards his car. As he neared his Range Rover, Douglas suddenly stopped in his tracks and wheeled round, heading straight back to the crime scene.

"Give me that fuckin' dog."

Grabbing Muffin's leash from Whitelaw, he led the spaniel into the back seat of his car and headed back to Bellshill.

\*\*\*\*\*\*\*\*\*\*\*\*\*\*\*\*\*\*

"What the fuck is that racket?" Hondo jumped out of his chair, knees knocking a half-full bottle of Miller off the coffee table. Hondo had fallen asleep in front of Sky News, hoping that they'd cover some of the incident at Chubbs' house. Having awoken to the sound of his door being hammered, polis-style, he was unimpressed and the good mood initiated by Chubbs' death vanished instantly.

Hondo checked the wee clock in the corner of the TV screen: 23:15

*Fuckin' Stevie!*

He recognised that bastard's door-thumping. Swearing machine-gun style as he unlocked the door, Hondo angrily grabbed the handle and yanked, revealing DCI Diller and Muffin standing on his 'Welcome' doormat. DCI Diller looked pretty pissed, even more so than he had on the TV earlier.

All anger replaced by confusion and mild amusement, Hondo greeted the pair.

"Officers," he exclaimed cheerfully, regarding both Douglas and Muffin. "What can I do for you handsome men this fine night?"

Without answering, Douglas shoved past Hondo, leading Muffin into the living room. The pair of Strathclyde Police's finest proceeded to search each room of Hondo's house together, DCI Miller sniffing away as much as the dog was, his copper's senses tuned to max. *David had called it 'Dad's Spidey-sense' when he'd been a wee kid.*

"Come on now, Detective Chief Inspector. If you've no warrant, this is an illegal search and anything discovered is inadmissible." Hondo smiled his predator's smile at Douglas. Muffin snarled at Hondo. "Your wee dug looks like an arsehole to me, Dougie."

"Ha. He is that," Douglas laughed humourlessly before continuing upstairs, ignoring Hondo's presence.

Muffin led him around the whole house, sniffing away, giving signals when nearby old man Crosbie's chair in Hondo's bedroom and in young Lionel's room. All they discovered was a few fine grains of coke in the old man's chair and Lionel's personal cannabis stash.

"What did ye expect, Dougie?" Hondo asked cheerfully. "A pile of cocaine just sitting, waiting for you to find it on the kitchen table? You could have found a fuckin' skip full of Charlie and you'd still have been fucked without a warrant."

Still silent, Douglas followed Muffin through to another corridor. The dog stopped in front of a locked door and began displaying very strong signals.

"Is Lionel in tonight?" Douglas asked.

You just missed him, Dougie. I'll tell him you're asking after him, will I?" Hondo motioned to the door in a *get the fuck out* gesture.

Douglas ignored the hint and nodded at the door Muffin seemed so interested in. "Where does this door go, Hondo?"

Laughing, Hondo rested his back against the door, blocking it. "None of your business, DCI Diller. Bring a warrant and I'll open it up for ye, but until then, you and yer wee dug can fuck right off."

Missing Hondo by centimetres, Douglas slammed his foot against the door, parallel to where the lock sat. The door exploded inward, swinging out over a staircase.

"A basement, eh?" Douglas asked, throwing Hondo another tight grin.

Hondo sighed and followed DCI Diller downstairs.

Emerging in the brightly-lit basement, Douglas immediately saw four pallets stacked high with shrink-wrapped bundles of literally and metaphorically dirty cash. Dirty from the hands it had passed through, it awaited a good cleaning, no doubt destined to be laundered at Green Billy's.

"You've been a busy big cunt, Hondo," Douglas sneered, patting the closest pile to him.

Hondo lobbed a Marlborough Red at Douglas and lit one for himself. Dougie had placed his cigarette in his mouth and motioned for a light. Hondo stretched out his arm as Douglas tilted his head to the side and placed his cigarette tip over the flame, eyes never leaving Hondo's for a second.

Walking past Douglas, Hondo gave the DCI a gentle shoulder, pushing him against the money. Coming to the rear-most pallet in the room, Hondo crossed one leg over the other and leaned his elbow on the stack of cash.

"Doesn't matter how busy I've been, Dougie. What we have right here is an illegal search. So you've seen all this cash, so what? You've fucked yourself by entering without a warrant. We're done here."

Douglas took a long drag on his Marlborough and blew the smoke up into the stark fluorescent strip-lights above, watching it swirl around in the light's heat for a second. Scanning around the room, he noted Hondo's Bowie knife protruding from his workbench, surrounded by playing cards.

"Still playing the cowboy, Hondo? At your age?" Douglas raised his eyebrows in a mocking gesture.

Tipping his Stetson arrogantly, Hondo stood tall once more and jabbed his thumb at the staircase. "Time for you two to go."

"Aye," Douglas told him, nodding and crushing the butt of his cigarette under his shoe. "I'll do that, but first I'll have to radio for some backup. We'll need a good few officers to clear all this shite up." Douglas pointed his index finger at the piles of currency to punctuate his words.

"You're living in a dream world, Douglas. No warrant, remember? All this is inadmissible."

Dougie smiled once more, a genuine smile this time.

"Only if I entered your property to perform a search, not if I came in here because I feared for someone's life, perhaps a fire or something." Douglas fished a petrol lighter out from his pocket. On the side it bore the legend, 'Fuck Communism'. David had bought it for him one Father's Day, said it was memorabilia from some comic he'd read. From his inside jacket pocket Douglas removed his hip flask and poured Russian Standard Vodka from it over the nearest pile of money.

"There's a lot of paper in here, Hondo, all packed in tight, close together."

Hondo's face was iron. "I don't want to have to kill ye, Dougie. That'd be... inconvenient for me. Just go home."

Douglas smiled wider, delight and hate dancing in his eyes he sparked up his lighter and dropped it onto the wet surface. Hondo had mistaken DCI Diller for a man who wanted him convicted. Douglas didn't want that. Right now he wanted this animal in a cell, out of harm's way, if only for a while.

Hondo ran at Douglas, all fists and feet. For an arsehole, Muffin, all credit to him, was insanely loyal to his masters and got a grip of Hondo's right shin mid-swing, yanking so hard that the big man crashed heavily to the concrete basement floor. Douglas gave Hondo a boot in the balls to keep him there. Scratching Muffin behind the ear, "Well done wee man," he casually placed his right knee on Hondo's chest, pinning him to the floor. Voice dripping with hatred and venom, Douglas spoke quietly, pronouncing each word deliberately, his voice like gravel. "Stay the fuck away from my son."

Feeling Hondo try to move, Douglas smashed his forehead down onto the big man's nose, breaking it and knocking him out.

Fifteen minutes later, Douglas had dragged Hondo up to the main house and out onto the grass where he lay unconscious next to his Harley. Douglas turned to the house, noting that the fire had followed them out of the basement and had begun licking along the walls in the hallway. He reentered the house, woke Hondo's dad and escorted him out onto the front lawn. The old man sat chuckiling, watching the flames. Confident that the cash would be cinders by now, he retrieved his radio, called for a fire engine and then a van to take Hondo into custody.

"Saved your life, big man."

Still out cold, Hondo didn't respond.

"Ungrateful bastard," Douglas laughed.

Watching Muffin sniff around the downed drug dealer, Douglas lit another cigarette and watched Muffin cock a leg to take a piss on Hondo's chest.

Strolling over to tickle the dog, Douglas told him, "Ach you're no' an arsehole after all, eh Muffin?" and then joined the fun.

# FRIDAY

Mark Wilson

# Chapter 16

## Opportunity Knocks

Stuffing toast into his mouth, Diller sat on the couch in his mum's living room trying to take in everything that had happened the night before. By 10:30 am the news reports from Hoylake Park were still coming through. *Murder, Mr Bowie, DCI Diller.* Sitting enjoying his second breakfast of the day, Diller swung between worrying, laughing and sitting bewildered at the previous day's events.

Douglas had been at work since nine on Thursday morning and was still dealing with the case now. Diller had texted his dad for updates a few times and had gotten the distinct impression that Douglas was under tremendous stress. Currently his dad sat at Bowie's bedside, power-napping, waiting for the old man to wake up. Diller had no idea why his dad had taken the case so personally, but it made him nervous all the same.

Despite his incredulity at the drama that had played out, Diller found that his mind kept returning to the question of what Bowie had been doing at Chubbs' place. It was too much of a coincidence that

Mr Bowie had been there at the same time as Diller had. *Why would he even be there? Did he know Chubbs?*

The answer came rushing at him suddenly. *He followed me.*

Mr Bowie had brandished his notebooks at Diller a few times in school. *It's all in here, Mr Diller, all in here.*

Diller hadn't thought twice about Mr Bowie's notebooks, considering them the product of a man with a chip on his shoulder and too much time on his hands. He'd figured, *so what if he logs me in and out of school in his wee book, he'll just come across as vindictive and petty to anyone he shows it to.*

Diller had to face another possibility. W*hat if he's been following me around outside of school too? Was it even possible that this cranky, arthritic old cunt has been following me? What would it mean?* He'd be royally fucked, that's what.

No longer laughing, Diller was on his feet and out the door. He always thought better when moving on foot. It was obvious that the notebooks either hadn't been found or didn't mention his name, otherwise he'd have been picked up by now. The police reports had mentioned that Bowie's prints were on the knife, and there was blood all over him. They had more than enough evidence to charge him with murder, but when Bowie woke up, or when his notebooks turned up, the police would have a much more obvious witness in Diller, especially if his books noted Diller's presence at Chubbs' on the night of his murder.

He had to find the notebooks and then see what he could do about getting to Bowie before he began talking, if he even woke up. On top of that, he had Hondo to deal with; it was Friday, after all. *Fuck it. Hondo can wait, I need to get myself out of this shit first, otherwise Hondo might just be doing me a favour by offing me before this day's done.*

Having already called Miss Davidson at the school office to call in sick once again, Diller was surprised to hear a voicemail beep through from the school as he strode along Sutherland Place towards Bowie's home. Miss Davidson had left a short message for him.

"David, I'm sorry to call you when you're still sick at home, but Mr McLatchie needs to see you urgently, before the weekend. He's asked if you can come in later today after you've rested a bit. He'll be here until six pm. Mr McLatchie stresses that it's urgent. Thanks David, bye."

Diller cut off the message and pocketed his phone, wondering if the gods had chosen today as his own personal hell.

Reaching Bowie's home, Diller noted that the police teams had already been and gone. This was a blessing and a curse. He was glad they'd been as the chance that someone might find him raking through Bowie's house was greatly reduced. This did present the possibility that they now had Bowie's notebooks sitting in the bottom of an evidence box, waiting for someone to examine them.

Diller slipped through the side gate and into the back yard. Trying the doors and windows, he discovered that the kitchen window was slightly ajar and he was inside the house in moments. Moving from room to room, Diller pulled out items and carefully returned them. He searched every square inch of Bowie's house over the course of two hours and found nothing.

Mind racing, Diller left Bowie's house. Taking a short-cut through the Barratt houses, and passing Lawmuir Primary School, Diller climbed up the old coal Bing and began winding his way along the side of the little hill which faced Footfield Road. Diller could see Hondo's house from his elevated position and was surprised to see the front door's frame blackened by fire. The Bowie situation still pressed, but an idea itched Diller's brain.

Lying flat on his stomach he peered into Hondo's house and called the house number. After two rings, Lionel picked up.

"Hullo? Dad?"

Diller grinned. "It's not yer daddy, Lionel."

"You're a sick bastard. What the fuck have you done with him?" Lionel screeched.

Letting Lionel rant for a few moments, Diller allowed himself a little time to figure out where to take the conversation. He'd expected to get Hondo on the phone, not Lionel, but from his reaction it was obvious that all was not well at Chez Crosbie. *Could Hondo be in trouble?* Lionel obviously thought something had happened to his dad.

Deciding to take a gamble, Diller growled into the phone, "Shut the fuck up, dumbass. I've got yer da. If you want him back get yourself to the place I had my last manicure." Diller hung up and watched Lionel storm out of the house leaving the front door flapping. He straddled Hondo's Harley and took off towards Motherwell Road and Dalzell steelworks.

Opening his contacts again, Diller selected Stevie's number. "Stevie, I'm in Dalzell steelworks and Lionel's after me," he screeched into the phone and pushed the disconnect button before Stevie could answer. Diller grinned and descended the coal Bing. Walking straight into Hondo's house he called himself a cab, directing it to pick him up from Lawmuir School and to take him to the Our Lady of Good Aid Cathedral. Close enough to the steelworks without placing him at the scene.

Bowie would have to wait; Lionel had now moved to the top of his queue. Diller checked his phone: 13:15.

# Chapter 17

## Lanarkshire Steelmen

**13:30**

Pain shot from Douglas's foot, up the back of his calf and through his hamstrings, culminating in a twinge in his lower back intense enough to make him straighten his leg and swear loudly in response. Douglas had been sleeping in the large chair with his feet up on Bowie's bed for around two hours. His sciatica was bearable for the most part, but it made one hell of a wake-up call. Rising to his feet and stretching his back a few times, Dougie made his way over to Bowie and checked him for signs of movement. *Nothing.* Duncan Bowie hadn't so much as twitched all night.

The cardiac surgeon, who'd been monitoring the old man, had told Dougie that Bowie's heart attack had been severe, and the result of a blockage in his coronary artery. The doctor was more concerned with Mr Bowie's stroke. A neurosurgeon had been to see Bowie several times and both doctors agreed: the next twenty-four hours would be critical. "He may never recover, DCI Diller," the weary-faced Cardiac man had informed him.

Mark Wilson

DCI Diller had dumped Hondo in a cell the previous night and made straight for Wishaw General. The longer Douglas had spent staring at the unconscious Bowie throughout the night, the more frustrated he'd become. The more he'd grown to hate the man for betraying his son, for spying on him.

There were simply too many things the he didn't know. *Why has this man been following David? Did he really see Hondo abduct him, and if so why? What did Hondo want with my son?*

And then there was the question he almost didn't want an answer to. *Was David at Francesco Valenti's house on Wednesday night? Is that how Bowie came to be there?*

Dougie had been going round in circles in his mind for most of the night, trying to figure out the answers, but had gotten nowhere so far. The vindictive old man resting on the bed was the only one who knew, but he wasn't saying a word.

Hearing his phone vibrating roughly in his jacket pocket, Douglas strolled over to the chair where it hung and retrieved it.

"DCI Diller, what can…"

"Dougie, it's Stevie Miller," Stevie interrupted. "You were right, your Davie's in trouble. I need you now. The Dalzell steelworks, move."

Douglas fished his car keys from his pocket and ran from the building to his Range Rover. Screeching from the car park, lights and siren blazing, he heard only his own heart thumping in his ears.

********

"Just gie me the fuckin' Jiffy bag," Hondo roared at Whitelaw.

"Sir," Whitelaw said with heavy condescension, "we have procedure we have to follow."

"Right, hurry up then," Hondo sighed, rapping his fist on the counter for emphasis.

Whitelaw raised an eyebrow and turned his attention back to his list. "Belt, brown leather. Cigarette lighter with confederate flag…"

Hondo again sighed loudly but failed to hurry Whitelaw along. Accepting that he'd have to allow the young copper to go through the motions, Hondo leaned over the desk, resting his face in his hands and his elbows on the desk.

He could hear his phone buzzing away inside the Jiffy bag that they always kept your personal items in when you were banged up.

Considering what could have happened last night, and apart from losing so much cash, Hondo felt lucky that despite Dougie Diller's gung-ho arrest, there really wasn't anything that they could hold him on. Dougie wasn't stupid. He must've known that Hondo would be back on the streets in a matter of hours. That also meant that he knew that Davie was in the shit and had wanted time to assess the situation.

Hondo realised that there was no way that Dougie knew anything about his son's *night job*. Young Davie was far too careful. Something *had* got Dougie good and riled, though. Perhaps one of the wee scallies he'd picked up had mentioned Hondo's interest in Dougie's son. He couldn't know.

Hondo couldn't really blame Dougie for the measures that he'd taken, burning his cash and dragging him off to the cells. Any father would do the same if he thought his son were in danger. The thought of a son being hurt is a powerful and devastating incentive. He could almost forgive Dougie's actions for that reason. Monday's conversation with his sister itched at the back of his mind.

But forgiveness wasn't an option for Hondo. There was no opportunity to bring the young Diller in line now. Dougie had left him no other recourse: Dougie and Davie both had to go. It would be problematic, getting rid of a high-profile CID officer and his son, but not impossible.

Whitelaw finally completed his bureaucracy five minutes later. Snatching his belongings up, Hondo rocketed through the blue double doors of the station out onto Thorn Road. Feeling his phone vibrate, Hondo noted that the screen displayed twenty-five missed calls from Lionel. Unlocking the phone, Hondo selected the most recent voicemail and held it to his ear.

"Dad, I've been looking for you all night. You weren't home when I got back. I just got a call telling me that you're being held at the Steelworks. I called you in case he's lying... God I hope he's lying. I'm going to kill this bastard, Dad."

Hondo ended the call at that and, not for the first time in the last twenty-four hours, took a second or two to wonder what the fuck was going on.

According to his phone, Lionel had left him that message five minutes ago. It was 13:35 now.

He reached the steelworks in ten minutes.

*********

Stevie hopped out of the cab in Park Street, right in front of the steelworks. Looking along the road to the security cabin and its road barriers, Stevie noted that there were no workers around. This wasn't unusual. The works had been operating on a half-day Friday rota for several years now. Scanning around, his eyes were drawn up to the Dalzell sign, white on a blue background. Years ago there had been loads of these signs scattered around the various steelworks, now only Dalzell remained.

Continuing slowly around the main building, Stevie moved towards the large, hangar-type grey and blue building at the rear of the yard. *If anyone's here, that's where they'll be*, he thought as he hugged close to walls and slipped around fences, eventually making his way to the rear of the building.

Stevie approached a small door cut inside one of the larger hanger doors. As the door lay ajar, he poked his head in and checked inside. Slipping in, Stevie hugged the walls some more, making his way around the inside perimeter of the building.

The building stank of rust and metal. Every little shuffle of his feet echoed off the metal walls as he tried to creep through undetected. The place seemed empty. There was no sign of Davie or Lionel.

Letting out a long sigh, Stevie stepped away from the wall he'd been leaning against, intending to walk back to where he'd entered. Suddenly Lionel shot out from some machinery he'd been crouching behind. Huge wrench in hand, he swung hard and split Stevie's skull with a heavy blow just above his left ear.

Stevie twitched for a few seconds, forming a grotesque version of a snow angel in the deep metallic dust of the workshop floor, whilst Lionel stood and watched. A few moments later, Lionel joined Stevie in the decades of filth of the floor, quite dead.

# Chapter 18

## Steel Yourself

**13:40**

Diller stalked around the two men on the floor, taking a wide, circular sweep. Sneering at them, he flicked his wrist, splatting the blood from the blade he'd just plunged into Lionel's brain stem onto Stevie's chest. Lionel lay face down, a foot to the right of Stevie who was on his back, muscles still twitching, pinned down with fear and pain. The blow to Stevie's head had obviously done some damage. It was clear that he saw Diller standing over him, but didn't seem able to move, apart from the twitching.

Diller slid his eyes analytically around the room, checking for anyone else's presence. Deciding that they were alone, he turned his attention to Lionel. He'd promised Lionel that he'd suffer for torturing him. He'd promised him that in the very room they were in now, but Lionel was dead and about to serve his needs in a different manner. With some effort he turned Lionel over and slid his knife under Lionel's neck, pulling up and towards himself, in his favourite vertebrae-severing cut. Of course Lionel didn't need to be incapacitated; this time he was cutting for another reason.

When he'd completed the vertebrae cut, he switched to his smaller knife and removed Lionel's left eye, followed by his finger tips and toes. Diller then used the butt of his blade to smash most of Lionel's teeth to rows of craggy, jagged shards.

This was how he habitually prepared his victims' bodies for burning and then burial. This was his home, the act of murder. The only place where he felt truly real, truly alive.

Cocking his head to the side, Diller looked straight at Stevie, his eyes scanning and evaluating ex-DS Steven Miller. Crouching beside him, he examined his friend's head wound. Unwrapping the heavy duty tape from around the handles of his knives, Diller wiped the clean-looking handles of any trace of himself and slid one blade into each of Stevie's hands. *There, nice and tidy... well, almost.*

Looking at Stevie's wound, it seemed unlikely that he would survive, but unlikely wasn't certain enough for Diller. Slipping a pocket-sized, folded map into Stevie's trouser pocket, and taking Stevie's mobile, Diller then turned his attention to retrieving the wrench that Lionel had used on Stevie's skull. With gloved hands, Diller matched the head of the wrench to the shape of the wound on Stevie's head, and pushed the matching head deep into Stevie's brain tissue. Watching the accusing, betrayed look in Stevie's eyes fade and life leave him, Diller released the wrench, allowing it to drop with a clang.

Turning to leave, Diller heard a man's voice: his father's voice. Hondo was there also, and the two of them were coming in though the main door. As the heavy chains dragged the corrugated steel door higher, Diller quickly launched himself out through the door that Stevie had used to enter the hangar minutes before.

Once outside the building, Diller realised that if his dad was here, then Mr Bowie must be alone. It was tempting to take Hondo's motorbike, but he didn't want to alert Hondo and Douglas that anyone else had been at the steelworks. Things were tidy inside; best to leave it that way. As he turned to jog silently away, he heard an animal roar come from Hondo as, presumably, he discovered his son's mutilated body. Diller's heart and step lightened. Searching for a cab he thought to himself, *Maybe it's my lucky day after all.*

Mark Wilson

# Chapter 19

## Fathers and Sons
**13:45**

Screeching to a halt at the steelwork's traffic barriers, Dougie's Range Rover narrowly avoided ramming a black cab which at that moment had pulled up to the barrier. Recognising the cab's passenger, Douglas tore out of his car and straight towards the rear passenger door of the cab. Yanking it open, he launched into the rear of the cab, grabbed Hondo by the lapels and dragged him through the door onto the gravelly ground.

"Where the fuck is he?" he growled at Hondo.

Instantly up and back on his feet, Hondo shoved hard at Douglas, using both hands on the DCI's chest.

"I'm here for Lionel, Dougie. Back off."

Douglas screwed his face, trying to make sense of the situation. "You just got here?"

"Aye," said Hondo. "I got a phone message from my Lionel, saying that someone had told him to come here, that I was here and in danger."

Douglas used his eyes to scan around the building's perimeter from where they stood. As he assessed the area, his mind raced. *Is David in here? Has Lionel got him? Is Hondo setting me up?* Douglas simply couldn't know.

Deciding that Hondo looked as concerned as he himself did, he made the only choice a father could.

"Right, Hondo. Follow my lead. Can you do that?"

Hondo, face rigid, eyes worried, gave him a sharp nod.

Douglas reached into the trunk of his Range Rover and pulled out an aluminium baseball bat. "Let's go then," he told Hondo.

Approaching the hangar building from the front, the men exchanged instructions back and forth. As they reach the main door a loud clang rang out.

"Let's get in there," Douglas cried. "Go get that chain and yank the door up."

Hondo had already begun to move towards the corrugated door. Pulling at the chain, he grunted, "Get ready, Dougie."

The heavy door slid up quickly allowing both men to shoot through. Douglas placed his arm in Hondo's path in a *go easy* gesture, but the big man barrelled through. Seconds later he wished he hadn't.

In an area to the right of the centre of the large building, the two men found the blood-soaked bodies of ex-DS Miller and Lionel Crosbie. Within seconds

Douglas had gone into automatic pilot, circling the area, stepping lightly, mentally photographing every horrific detail of the scene. Stevie was dead, a cavernous section of his skull gone. Young Lionel was now in his father's arms. Hondo had slid his legs under his son's body, dragged him up towards him by the armpits and was cradling Lionel, arms wrapped around his son's large chest. He was also howling. A guttural sound, long and filled with timeless pain. The pain a parent feels when they outlive their baby.

Hondo was lost in his grief and allowed Douglas to move around him and Lionel, taking a mental note of wounds and maimings. Pulling on latex gloves, Douglas gently handled Lionel's hands, his feet, his lips and neck, examining the wounds that Stevie had inflicted, his *Spidey-sense* tingling away the whole time. Dougie's eyes flicked up to meet Hondo's every few seconds, checking he could continue, asking permission to examine Hondo's dead son. Hondo's eyes were bottomless pits of pain, defeat and grief. He looked, he was, utterly broken.

Douglas came around to where Stevie lay. Following the same procedure, he made his way around Stevie's body. His head had a hole the size of a fist above his left ear. Douglas could see the meninges of his brain, blackened and indented. Continuing methodically around, noting the blades in Stevie's hands, he discovered the map that David had placed in Stevie's pockets and a small wrap of coke. Nothing else.

Douglas sat on the cold, filthy floor and hugged his knees. There was no changing the facts. Every piece of evidence he'd scanned in the scene told him that Stevie had tortured and killed Young Lionel. The boy must've got a blow in, killing Stevie as he himself fought for life. It was a scene straight out of a horror movie. If someone had described it to him, he'd never have believed that his old friend was capable of the carnage before him, but here it was, right in front of him.

Unfolding the map, Douglas flicked his eyes over the single-sided sheet. It was a map of Strathclyde Park, with red circles marked in various locations, mostly in the woods. Douglas felt coldness shiver up his sciatic nerve as he counted forty-two red circles, and stood up to shake it off.

Douglas crouched once more across from Hondo who was utterly lost in grief. "Hondo," Douglas said gently. The big drug dealer was too far gone. "HONDO!" he shouted.

Like he was waking from a dream, and not a pleasant one, Hondo's red eyes looked across at Douglas. "Helen told me. She was right. Should've got out... My boy."

Douglas looked at Hondo who seemed to have aged a decade in the last few minutes and saw nothing left of the Hondo that he knew in the broken man's eyes.

"What did you want with my son?" Douglas asked the old man softly.

Hondo closed his eyes and choked down some self-loathing.

*I wanted to kill the son of a bitch. He's a filthy drug-dealing bastard, your son; he's a sadistic animal; he's worse than me!* He wanted to scream these words at Dougie, but what was the use.

None of it mattered now that Lionel was gone. He was finished. Looking at his son's vacant eye socket, Hondo decided that he wouldn't rob Douglas of *his* son, in thought or in deed.

"We picked him up to frighten you, Dougie, to make you back off a little. I've nothing against your David. You'll get no more bother from me." Nodding at Lionel's body, he whispered to Douglas. "It's over. I'm done."

With that, Hondo returned to rocking his son's body and wailing.

Douglas nodded. Satisfied that it was over, he stood and put a call into the station. Once a forensics team and several other officers had arrived at the scene, Douglas stepped outside, lit a cigarette and checked his watch: 14:30.

*David!* Fishing out his phone, Doulas called his son. Expecting that he was still in school, he didn't expect a reply but David picked up after a few rings.

"Are you ok, son. Are you in school?"

"Eh, no, dad. I phoned in sick today." David went quiet for a few seconds, a sure sign that he had something he didn't want to say. "I'm at Wishaw General, Dad."

"Why the hell are you there?"

"Why wouldn't I be here? I know that they're saying on the news that Mr Bowie killed someone, but c'mon Dad, I know him better than that."

*He doesn't know that Duncan Bowie's been following him.*

Douglas took a deep drag from his cigarette, blew the smoke through his nose and flicked the butt into the gutter. Steeling himself, he asked his son, "Where were you on Wednesday night, David?"

"At Gerry Malone's place. Spent the night there, Dad. Why?"

Relief surged through Douglas. Gerry Malone was one of Diller's mates from Angel's. A decent guy, with a good job.

"Thanks son, it doesn't matter why. Look, I don't want you visiting Mr Bowie, I don't want you anywhere near him at all. He's not the man you think that he is."

"What's going on, Dad?"

Douglas shook his head and continued. "Mr Bowie's been involved in some bad things with some bad people. He's not stable, David. He's been following you around, keeping notebooks."

David had gone silent on the other end of the phone, no doubt taking it all in.

"It's ok, David, the books are just a load of shite about you being in this place or that. No real harm in them, if a little concerning."

Douglas heard David laugh nervously. "I knew he did that in school, Dad, but he followed me about, everywhere I went? Why?"

"Dunno, son. We'll have to ask him when he wakes up."

More silence.

"That's not going to happen, Dad. Mr Bowie died a few minutes ago."

Douglas sat on a short wall behind him and let out a long breath that he hadn't realised he'd been holding.

"Right, David. I want you to go into school later, you're obviously not that ill. Go and see Mr McLatchie and let him know what's been happening.

I'll have called him by the time you see him, but he should hear your story, ok?"

"That's fine, Dad. I have a meeting with him later anyway."

"Right. I've got to crack on. I'll speak to you later. Love you, son."

"Love you too, Dad."

Douglas lit another cigarette and walked around to the main door to watch Hondo climb into the back of a police car, whilst his son was loaded into the back of a mortuary van. They'd both gone into that building at odds with each other, he and Hondo, but two fathers united nonetheless, worried for their sons. Less than an hour later and there was no longer any conflict between the two of them and only Douglas was a father.

Despite their shared history and years of animosity, Douglas's heart almost broke when he thought of the pain and guilt that Hondo must be feeling.

Sucking the last from his cigarette, DCI Diller unfolded the map he'd found on Stevie's body and shivered once again. When he'd examined young Lionel's body, Douglas had been shaken, more shaken than he could let Hondo see. It wasn't the process that had given him the creeps, he'd examined bodies many times before. He'd shuddered because he had seen identical wounds to Lionel's before, five years ago on a corpse found in a close on Lawmuir Road.

Douglas straightened his suit and climbed into his Range Rover. Radioing HQ for another forensics team, he screeched out of the steelworks towards Strathclyde Park.

# Chapter 20

## "Goodbye Mr Bowie"
### 14:15

The traffic had been a complete nightmare en route to Wishaw General from the steelworks. Combined with taking Diller some time to find a cab, it'd taken him almost half an hour to reach the hospital. On arrival, he'd slipped through the main doors and headed straight for the hospital's intensive care unit. Deciding that there was no point in trying to conceal his presence, he made his way directly to the front desk and asked for Mr Bowie's room.

"He's in 4D," the receptionist told him, "but DCI Diller has said absolutely no visitors."

Diller reached across the desk. Taking the receptionist's hands he forced grief into his voice and tears into his eyes. "DCI Diller's my dad, that man in there works in my school and was my teacher for years. I need to see him."

The nurse's bored expression softened. "You have any ID?"

Diller hid a grin as he produced his wallet, showing her his bank card.

She read the name carefully. "OK, David, but you'll have to be supervised. A nurse will accompany you, and no more than five minutes."

The gratitude he showed her was real. "Thanks so much," he sneaked a quick look at her name tag, "Daphne. You're a star."

Daphne threw him a tired smile and pointed towards Bowie's room.

"Over there, David. Nurse Fletcher's in there already, she'll supervise."

Mr Bowie lay covered from foot to neck in crisp, white blankets. Only his arms lay on top of the covers along with his bald, wig-free head. A number of wires trailed in and out of various orifices and across his chest. He was silent, except for gentle breaths rasping in and out of his lungs with the aid of a respirator. Diller squeezed some tears out for Nurse Fletcher's benefit as she motioned for him to take a seat next to Bowie's bed.

Looking at Bowie, Diller found it hard to believe that it was the same man who'd made his days at school a misery. It was the first time Diller had seen his face so relaxed and wearing a soft mask of peacefulness; normally his ever-present scowl dominated. Diller found himself thinking, *He'd be fairly handsome if he smiled.* Mr Bowie had begun torturing Diller when he'd been a fifth year at the school, but he'd really gone into overdrive when Mr McLatchie had named him Head Boy for the year. Bowie had always spat the name Head Boy at him with contempt, using it like an insult.

Nurse Fletcher placed a hand gently on his shoulder. "You should talk to him. Coma patients like it."

Diller shook his head. "I wouldn't know what to say." *I'd much rather shove a pillow over the old cunt's face, darlin'.* Diller truly didn't know what to do. There was no opportunity to dispose of Bowie, even discreetly. Even if Nurse Fletcher left him alone with Mr Bowie, too many people had seen him come in here. His only option was to wait. It would be Bowie's word against his when he awoke. It wasn't an ideal situation, but due to the manner in which Mr Bowie had been found at Chubbs' house, compounded by the fact that Douglas had evidence that he'd been stalking his son, Diller was confident that he'd be able to keep the coming investigation on Bowie alone. Still, it'd make keeping his business running almost impossible.

"Go ahead, David. I'll stand over here and give you a little privacy."

Nurse Fletcher made her way to the doorway. Standing just outside the open door, she placed herself in a position where she could see, but not hear.

Something shifted inside Diller's heart and he allowed his true self to rise to the surface. Bringing his lips close to Mr Bowie's ear, he whispered softly to him, like a lover.

"So you've been following me, eh Mr Bowie? You're full of surprises aren't you, ya vicious old cunt."

Diller moved his left hand and folded it gently around Mr Bowie's, for Fletcher's benefit.

"You found the little mess I left behind in Fran's house, didn't you? You must have shit yourself with excitement. You had me. I'd have been fucked, Mr Bowie. All you had to do was lift a phone and call the police." The fingers on Bowie's right hand twitched slightly.

"Everyone would have called you a hero. You'd have shown them all. But your rancid old fuckin' heart couldn't handle the excitement, eh? Tell them what you like when you wake up. No one will believe you. If only you could've made that call."

Diller stood. Taking Bowie's face in his left hand, he cradled it and brought his cheek in against Mr Bowie's, whispering once more.

"Fran was nothing. I've killed dozens. I'm worse than you ever thought it was possible for a human to be, and you could've stopped me."

Eyelids, crusted closed with sleep, began to flutter.

"War hero, lifelong teacher. No one will remember you as those things; everyone will spit your name when they say it. If they remember you at all. I wonder how many former pupils will turn up on the news. *He gave me the creeps. He touched me. I couldn't tell anyone before.* They always do, don't they? The attention seekers. You'll be branded an old creep, a paedo. Fuck you, Duncan."

Diller kissed Mr Bowie tenderly on the cheek and made for the door. As he thanked Nurse Fletcher, who was close to tears because of the tenderness of the exchange she'd witnessed, Mr Bowie began convulsing violently in his bed.

Standing aside, Diller watched the crash team charge into Bowie's room. Working with hands, chemical and defibrillators, the team fought to bring him back. They failed.

Nurse Fletcher was openly crying now. Diller was too, it was only decent after all, and he'd spent so much time practicing his fake tears he never missed an appropriate opportunity to use them.

Taking Diller in a tight embrace, Fletcher told him how sorry she was and eventually let him go.

"Do you want to call anyone?" she asked.

"Na," Diller sniffed, "I'm fine."

Diller's phone ringing interrupted the exchange. Checking the screen, he noted that it was his dad calling.

After a short exchange, during which his dad revealed that Bowie's notebooks wouldn't be a problem, Diller rung off and bolted to the nearest bathroom to conceal his joy. Nurse Fletcher watched him go and assumed that grief had hit him.

# Chapter 21

## Will The Real Davie Diller Please Stand Up!
## 17:30

Diller heard his phone beep and retrieved a message from his dad. 'Have been in Strathclyde Park all afternoon, son. Something huge has come up. Will be home late, we'll talk then. Love you.'

Noticing another message that had come from Hondo fifteen minutes before, Diller thumbed it open, and read it again for the tenth time. 'It's all yours, Davie. I'm retired. Had enough.'

Hondo had also emailed him a long list of contacts, shipments, bank account numbers and passwords, and assurances. Diller stuffed his phone in his pocket and smiled. Knocking gently on the heavy mahogany door, Diller waited until the little green light above the door to the head teacher's office blinked on and then entered.

Mr McLatchie, a huge bear of a man and a brilliant head teacher, was already halfway across the room, hand outstretched in greeting.

"David, come in, come in." Shaking the Rector's hand, Diller took a seat when invited to. "I'm so sorry to call you in here, when you've been sick, but by all accounts you've had yourself a busy time of it today."

Unsure what to say yet, Diller simply smiled and nodded.

Pulling a bottle of Bell's whiskey and two short glasses from his desk drawer, Mr McLatchie filled both glasses and slid one across to Diller. Eyeing it for a moment, Diller reclined back into his chair without reaching for the drink.

"Too strange for you, eh? Having a drink with the old head teacher?"

"Aye." Diller said. "Look, Mr McLatchie. What's this about?"

Mr McLatchie poured himself another measure and reclined back into his own, much bigger chair.

"DCI Diller called me today and told me about Mr Bowie's… extra-curricular activities." McLatchie looked very uncomfortable. "We had no idea that Mr Bowie was involved in anything illegal, David, and we certainly didn't know that he'd chosen to harass and stalk you inside and outside school."

Diller nodded. "I know, Mr McLatchie. It's been difficult, finding out that my mentor seemed to despise me."

"Yes," McLatchie said sadly. "You've worked together for, what is it? Ten years now."

Diller nodded, reaching for his drink after all.

McLatchie gave him a smile. "And the history you two shared. He taught you Higher English in fifth year when you were a pupil at the school, isn't that right?"

"Yeah, he called me 'Head Boy' as a nickname, even now."

"It must be very difficult to get your head around David, especially being there when he died this afternoon. What a myriad of emotions you must be dealing with."

Diller supressed a beaming smile.

*Only unbridled joy at present. Mr McL.*

"Yes," he said softly, bowing his head, all sorrow.

"Well, David," McLatchie announced in his booming Rector's voice. "We want you to know that you have our full support. As one of our own alumni and one of our brightest young teachers, we'd love for you to take Mr Bowie's post as Principal Teacher of English."

Diller gave McLatchie a genuine smile. "You would?"

McLatchie stood. Walking around to Diller's side of the desk, he sat on the edge and looked warmly down at him.

"Of course, David. You're an excellent teacher, one of the best we have. You've earned this promo-tion many times over and at thirty-eight you'd be our youngest ever Principal Teacher of English at the school... You're ideal for this position and in the circumstances, well, what better way for you to get some closure on everything that's happened recently and move on with your life."

Diller stood, bringing himself eye level with McLatchie. Pumping his hand in a firm shake, Mr David Diller, newly-minted PT of Bellshill Academy's English department beamed with genuine warmth and excitement.

"Right, well, I'll see you on Monday then, Mr Diller." McLatchie smiled at him, fetching this coat.

As Mr McLatchie walked Diller out into the car park, he asked him, "Got any plans for the weekend, David?"

"Oh, you know me Mr McLatchie. Always busy," Diller beamed.

\*\*\*\*\*\*\*\*\*\*

## Epilogue

**One Year Later**

# Serial-Killing Ex-Copper's Grave is Vandalised!

Hondo let out a long sigh when he read the headline on the front page of his *Daily Record*. He wondered at times like these why on earth he'd bothered to arrange shipment of his favourite paper to his new home in Miami at all.

"Have you seen this, Helen?" he asked his sister as she entered the room, carrying a margarita for each of them.

"It's a load of shite that newspaper, Jim. Here, there's your drink. Put that thing in the bin, finish your drink and we'll go for a swim."

For the first time in his life, Hondo had a deep, Florida tan and a peaceful demeanour. He'd never felt so at home, not in the steelworks and certainly not dealing coke. Helen had been spot on; she usually was. He should have done this years ago.

Taking a long pull on his margarita, Hondo looked down to the beach, fifty feet from the porch of their beach house, and thought of Lionel. *He'd have loved it here.* The thought was a lie; Lionel would've been miserable here. He'd have stuck out like a sore thumb and made no attempt to fit in. Even with the boy grumbling incessantly, Hondo desperately wished he could be there with him.

That bastard, Stevie. In the months following Lionel's murder, the police had found over forty bodies in various states of decomposition. The map that Dougie Diller had taken from his body, and the manner in which he'd killed Lionel, suggested strongly that Stevie had been killing for decades. Scotland's very own serial killer and an ex-copper to boot; it was a fascinating case and one which the UK media had frenzied over.

All that time spent worrying about Davie Diller and a truly psychopathic freak like Stevie had been playing him for years. DCI Diller had made a statement before he'd retired stating that he suspected that the killings began when Stevie had had his episode and left the police force. DCI Diller also told the press that he believed that the Strathclyde Police Force should have done more to assist former-DS Miller when his mental health deteriorated.

Since the news of the Lanarkshire Ripper, *what a fucking name to give him,* broke, dozens of customers and old slappers from Angel's had crawled out the woodwork to claim past scares at Miller's hands. His ex-wife had signed a book deal, a 'living with the ripper' type job. *Good luck to her,* Hondo thought. That poor lassie and her kid will be hounded their whole lives because of *him.*

Fran Valenti's murder had never resulted in any conviction being made against anyone. The teacher, Mr Bowie, had died in hospital within a day of Fran's murder and being the police's only suspect, they'd closed the case. From what Hondo had heard, with the media interest drawn to the Ripper case, the puzzle of Fran's apparent murder at Mr Bowie's hands was glossed over and forgotten about.

Hondo was happy to be away from it all. Diller had taken control of every aspect of his former empire, and he was welcome to it. Still, he had to give the boy some credit. How he managed to juggle Hondo's business and keep a respectable full-time job in the school, Hondo couldn't fathom. Davie had been graceful enough to send Hondo a quarterly check, a pension of sorts. In Hondo's view, that showed a bit of class. *Clever, lad.*

Finishing his margarita, Hondo smiled over at Helen. "Is Dad sleeping in the house?"

"Aye," Helen replied.

"Swim?" he asked.

"Aye."

**END**

**Look out for more great titles from Mark Wilson on <u>Amazon</u> and at <u>Paddy's Daddy Publishing</u>**

**Also By Mark Wilson:**

<u>Bobby's Boy</u>
<u>Naebody's Hero</u>

Mark Wilson

## You may also enjoy:

## <u>Life Is Local by Des McAnulty</u>

### *The Cult Debut Novel from Des McAnulty*

*Motherwell 2002. Whilst trying to come to terms with the bizarre suicide of his ex-girlfriend Clare, College student Stevie Costello dreams of a better life far away from his hum-drum existence. Before Stevie can change his life, he must first contend with his straight-laced boss Alastair, whose marriage to the breath-taking Marie is on the verge of collapse.*

*To further complicate things, Stevie finds himself somehow caught between best friends, Stubbsy and Lisa, whose hatred for each other explodes one night into an intoxicating love under a blazing Motherwell sun.*

*Can Stevie somehow shake off the shackles of his surroundings or will he finally realise that love and life really is local...*

*Inspired by the music of Mogwai, The Delgados and Morrissey; as well as James Kelman's 'How Late it Was How late' and James Robertson's 'The Testament to Gideon Mack'*

### *Praise for Life Is Local*

*"Des gives each character motives without judgement, merely explanation and leaves it to the reader to decide*

Mark Wilson

*on the characters' worth." - Mark Wilson, Author of*
*Naebody's Hero*

## Available now on Amazon

# Strangers are Just Friends You Haven't Killed yet

## By Ryan Bracha

What do you get if you cross a French sex addict hitman, a self-righteous left wing blogger with a spam problem, a racist bar room regular and his penchant for porn, an American gangster with a lot of reflecting to do, a small time journalist who dreams of the big time, a weak-willed loner with a Victorian lion hunter alter-ego, a flamboyant PR guru and his devilish plans, a very recently unemployed call centre drone, an old man with a hell of a grudge, and A LOT, of dead bodies? You get this.

The naked corpse of a young man is discovered with his throat sliced open on a cool autumn morning in a park in Sheffield, northern England. By an elderly dog-walker, as usual. He is the first of a rapidly increasing number of seemingly random killings in the city, all in that same way. This leads to a frenzy of media and public specu-lation, where everybody is a suspect, and every-body has an opinion. Daisy is pointing the finger at the media, rookie journalist David is dreaming of future awards for his coverage of the whole thing, and Terry blames the Asians.

What's actually happening is a far more sinister affair which threatens to spiral out of control.

Across the city Tom, call centre outlaw, cast out for his lack of respect for faceless voices, is drinking and snorting himself into a collision course with some very very bad people indeed, how it will end, well that depends on how much of an outlaw Tom's prepared to be.

Strangers Are Just Friends You Haven't Killed Yet is a funny, satirical, sexy, and very violent tale of poverty, addiction, the fickle finger of fame, love and questionable mental health.

Next time you'll maybe want to look that gift horse in the mouth.

**<u>Available now on Amazon</u>**

21921250R00129

Printed in Great Britain
by Amazon